THE MIDNIGHT ARROW

Copyright © 2025 by Zoey Draven
ISBN: 978-1-966810-00-1

All rights reserved.

This book is a work of fiction. Names, characters, places, and events are the product of the author's imagination. Any resemblance to actual events, places, or persons are purely coincidental.

No part of this book may be reproduced in any form or by any electronic or mechanical means, including information storage and retrieval systems, without written permission from the author, except for the use of brief quotations in a book review.

Cover Art by David Gardias

Editing by Mandi Andrejka at Inky Pen Editorial Services

For more information visit www.ZoeyDraven.com

ALSO BY ZOEY DRAVEN

Warriors of Luxiria
The Alien's Prize
The Alien's Mate
The Alien's Lover
The Alien's Touch
The Alien's Dream
The Alien's Obsession
The Alien's Seduction
The Alien's Claim

Horde Kings of Dakkar
Captive of the Horde King
Claimed by the Horde King
Madness of the Horde King
Broken by the Horde King
Taken by the Horde King
Throne of the Horde King

Warrior of Rozun
Wicked Captor
Wicked Mate

The Krave of Everton
Kraving Khiva
Prince of Firestones
Kraving Dravka
Kraving Tavak

Brides of the Kylorr
Desire in His Blood
Craving in His Blood

Hordes of the Elthika
The Horde King of Shadow

Standalones
Rescued by the Luxirian

THE MIDNIGHT ARROW

ZOEY DRAVEN

THE MIDNIGHT ARROW

"Tell me a secret, little witch."

Marion enjoys her quiet life of solitude in the shadowy woods of the Black Veil, where even the local villagers don't dare venture. She sells her healing potions at the village market by day and tends to her otherworldly garden by night, caring for her magical bees and furry familiar, Peek, at their cottage.

Then, one moonlit night, she encounters a devilishly handsome male—with powerful wings, sharp fangs, and high fae-like beauty—shot through with a lethal poisoned arrow.

Under her healer's oath, she's bound by magic to try to save the mysterious stranger. But as she nurses him back to health, she begins to suspect that Lorik Ravael isn't quite what he seems. He knows too much about the Black Veil, rumored to be the entrance to the Below, a realm of dangerous magic and soulless monsters. Yet she's drawn to him, bewitched by his luminous eyes, seductive grin, and silver tongue of riddles.

But as their forbidden desire ignites, she fears Lorik is hiding darker secrets than she imagined—secrets that could cost her a heart she isn't willing to give.

CONTENT CONSIDERATIONS

The Midnight Arrow contains some themes and depictions that might be sensitive to certain readers. Please go to my website for a full list of content considerations.

Scan this QR code for easy access:

CHAPTER 1

There was a dead glowfly poking out of the wrathweed hive.

The entrance hole, no bigger than a marble, was clogged up with its plump body. Outside, in the brisk night air, glowflies circled. Agitated and concerned. And if I wasn't careful, I might get stung. And if I got stung, I'd be bedridden for two days, even with the help of wrathweed to dilute the poison of their venom.

The light in the glowfly's body had burned out. I'd been noticing him for three nights, studying the way the cerulean blue in his translucent abdomen kept flickering.

"Let me help," I whispered, waving my hand in front of the hive in practiced, slow motions. The glowflies darted away, though they hovered close by, their wings silent as if they waited with bated breath.

I pinched the glowfly's large wings between my fingertips and gently pulled. His body popped from the entrance, and a stream of wrathweed glowflies wiggled themselves out in his absence.

I set him in the circle of my palm, thinking that I could grind his body into a powder once it dried out and use it in a sleeping potion for the market day. Then I sighed, the thought of a greedy tongue and loud swallow drinking his body down not sitting well with me.

I was the keeper of these glowflies—five different varieties. The *only* keeper of all five glowfly hives on Allavar, and there was a trust that pervaded all else, except perhaps in matters of life or death.

The wrathweed glowflies followed me to their section of the night garden, casting me in bright blue light with every hushed step on the soft green earth. I laid his body at the root of a smaller wrathweed plant and covered him in fragrant, black soil. I stared at the small lump he made as his hive mates fluttered past me, landing on the long, sturdy leaves of the plant. They shook their bodies, their blue dust covering the wrathweed, trickling to the soil beneath.

Then they flew off and went about their business…and I went about mine. Death was a natural part of this garden—an important part.

Dusting the soil off my hands, I picked up my gathering basket and walked to the fire-cup bed. The fire cup glowflies bled orange light through their bodies. If I closed my eyes, I could almost imagine it was the sun casting shadows over my lids—that was how brightly they burned.

"Harvest night," I announced. "So don't get cranky with me, you little heathens."

A fire cup glowfly whizzed past when I pulled out my shears, an inch away from my nose, its wings brushing my eyelashes.

I huffed but strode forward. Mercifully, though the fire cup glowflies were the most aggressive of my collection, their stings did only that—sting like fire. It was the wrathweeds' sting I needed to be wary of, though luckily, next to the shadevine glowflies, they were among the calmest of their species and didn't spook easily.

"Let's see how well you did this moon cycle, shall we?" I

asked, crouching down by my raised beds, my knees digging into the softened ground.

Inspecting a fire cup, I touched the velvety softness of its petals. The flower was the brightest of reds, and its golden-yellow stamens gleamed from the glowflies' magic. Streams of orange light pulsed from within the petal, like waves in a calm ocean.

"Beautiful," I declared, grinning, just as a glowfly landed on the back of my hand. I placed my shears an inch below the flower, snipping the stem cleanly. "Well done."

As if he understood my praise, my glowfly companion preened, letting out a small buzzing noise before darting away.

I harvested three additional fire-cup blooms, though this section of my garden was nearly full of them. I only needed three for the healing cream I would bottle and take to the market. The sale of them alone would be enough to pay for the materials to repair the eastern window of my cottage before winter. There might even be enough money left over for fabric to make a new dress, a warmer one.

It was nearing midnight when I finished tending to the garden. With the first bite of winter, the fire cups would begin to hibernate, as would their glowfly counterparts. Only the shadevine and the wrathweed would continue to produce during the snowy season. But I would need to start preserving the brightbell and the death needle before their last leaves dropped in the coming months.

Exiting my garden, I closed the squeaky waist-high gate behind me. With a lingering glance over my shoulder, I admired the myriad of colors the glowflies made as they weaved and buzzed, a vibrant and brilliant kaleidoscope of magic, like multi-colored shooting stars in an inky night sky.

When I reached the gray cobblestone path that led up to the door of my cottage, I stilled, my eyes snapping to the darkened forest beyond the edge of my property.

The glowflies' gentle humming ceased, and a chill went down my spine.

Being watched was not a new sensation. There was a reason no one dared to live in the Black Veil, the forest in which I'd made my permanent home like the crazy human fool I was, as the villagers often *tsked* at me on market day—Allavari, Kylorr, and Ernitians alike.

Fear was not a new feeling. I'd been afraid nearly my entire life.

But the Black Veil was the entrance to the Below. No one knew where it lay within the forest, just that the Severs roamed these woods and, occasionally, snatched a villager or two to take Below with them.

Severs had watched me before, their presence curious but ominous. I'd seen them between the trees—tall, dark, hulking shadows with their wingless bodies and bright, consuming eyes. Every single time had stabbed a shard of ice deep in my belly, but I knew the barrier spell around my property would be enough to keep them away—or so the Allavari witch assured me every moon cycle when I paid her hefty price to keep it fresh and charged.

There was a Sever out in the woods right then. Watching me. I could feel it, like the touch of death trailing along my flesh. I'd never seen one up close, only in illustrations and drawings, likely meant to scare village children. But truthfully, they scared me too. They scared many.

"Peek?" I called out, my voice wavering uncertainly. "Peek, where are you?"

A dark flash appeared in the corner of my eye, and I crouched down, keeping my gaze on the forest's edge, drawing the protection barrier's path in my mind's eye in reassurance.

Peek's slinking walk was agitated, his back slightly arched, black-and-indigo fur standing on end.

"I know," I said quietly, running my hand over his small furry head. He nuzzled into my hand even though his slitted eyes were fastened beyond the trees. He could see the Sever—I was certain of it. "Let's go inside for the night, all right? I don't want you out here."

I picked him up, his warm, small body a comfort against me, despite the stiffness of his limbs. Cradling the basket of fire cups, I turned my back on the forest, keeping my walk measured, and disappeared into my cottage, shutting the door with a heavy thud and sliding the bolt into place.

I closed the shutters on the windows, sealing us inside the brightly lit space. Then I waited with bated breath…

And I only let out a sigh of relief when I heard my glowflies begin to hum again.

"He's gone," I said, keeping my tone bright. "Are you hungry?"

Peek let out a warbling mew.

I smiled, though I was still a little shaken. "Midnight snack it is."

The bellow woke me.

So loud and startling that it felt like it'd been yelled directly into my ear.

My eyes flew open, and I flung back the heavy quilt, my heart racing, my mouth bone dry. After I scrambled to stand from my bed, I stood stock still, listening. I held my breath. I couldn't hear my glowflies in the back garden, but I could hear my cauldron bubbling in a light simmer, the fragrance of the spicy fire cups permeating my small cottage, stinging my nostrils.

When I crept out to the front room, I saw Peek, fur ruffled, staring directly at the closed door.

Another bellow came, freezing the breath in my lungs. It

sounded far off, echoing through the trees—certainly not as close as I thought it'd been.

"Peek, stay here," I murmured, grabbing the shawl draped across the seat of my cauldron's stool and wrapping it around my shoulders. My green nightdress swayed against my ankles as I shoved my feet into my worn leather boots.

The moon was full tonight, casting the forest in silver, so I didn't take my Halo orb to light my path. I did, however, grab my dagger and a pouch of finely ground fire-cup powder.

No one knew where the entrance to the Below was after all… or what happened to you once the Severs took you there. Just that you were never seen again.

Stepping out of my cottage, I took in a deep breath and exhaled, the crisp air fogging in front of me.

The bellow came again. Male. In pain.

Hurt, I thought, biting my lip.

By what? I wondered next.

I took to the path. It was difficult to track sound in the density of the forest, but I was fairly certain he was close.

My footsteps crunched over half-frozen fallen leaves, and twigs entwined in my hair from low branches, as if warning me to stay back. I cursed myself—*fool, fool, fool,* I thought—even as my legs propelled me forward, deeper and deeper into the forest.

But as a healer on Allavar, though I was human, I was honor bound to help those who needed it. Bound in blood and magic. Even strangers in the Black Veil on a moonlit night. It was in the oath I'd taken, the task granted to me when I'd passed my studies all those years ago.

His agonized moans and heavy breathing led me straight to him, farther north than I'd imagined but not so far from my cottage.

Peering through the trees, I finally spied him through the foliage and brush.

A Kylorr male, I realized, my heartbeat ticking up. One I recognized. From the village on market days. *Him.*

My cheeks flushed hot, the memory of those mischievous pale blue eyes spearing straight through my mind.

A breeze picked up through the trees, rustling my hair forward, and I watched his nostrils flare, his wings twitching. His gaze fastened straight on me, though he couldn't possible see me hidden in the darkness.

"I know you're there," came his deep voice, tinged in something darker. *Pain,* I realized. "I would know your scent anywhere, little witch."

He was sitting with his back against the trunk of an ancient tree, towering high overhead, its canopy disappearing into the night.

His skin was a lighter gray—almost silver—than other Kylorr I'd seen, and his features resembled the Allavari's sculpted elegance. High cheekbones, sharp enough to slice; a sloped nose I'd envision pressing my lips to more than once; and pointed ears that were decorated in silver piercings. His jaw held the unforgiving sharpness of a blade, and his lips were set in a small pout, his fangs *just* poking into his bottom lip since he sensed danger near.

The black horns that jutted from his temples curved around the crown of his head, sloping upward at the ends. His hair, silky black and long, hung below his shoulders, nearly to the middle of his back. The ends that covered his right shoulder looked wet.

Blood.

That was when I saw it.

A silver-tipped metal arrow was lodged deep in his chest. The shaft was glittering blue. A blue I recognized as trepidation made my belly lurch.

The Kylorr male had been shot with a poisoned arrow…and left to die in the Black Veil alone.

CHAPTER 2

"Show yourself," came the Kylorr's voice, cutting through the foggy haze in my mind.

Night nettle poison. The most beautiful of blues, shimmering like a sunlit ocean, and the last color many saw before it took their life quickly.

Ignoring his words, though unknowingly obeying them, I scurried from behind the tree. The Kylorr's eyes fastened on me, his jaw tightening. As I approached, his head tipped back against the tree he was propped up against so he could keep my gaze.

His long, finely muscled legs were sprawled out before him, and I sank down beside his right side, peering at the wound.

"There you are, little witch," he said, his voice warm and husky, even in his pain. "I hope I didn't wake you this night."

"Hush and let me think," I admonished, already running through the antidotes I had prepared. I always liked to have the antidote for night nettle in my storage chests—I just couldn't remember if I'd sold the last of it at the prior market day. I'd been waiting for the next crop of brightbell in my garden, but they grew twice as slowly as all the rest, even with the glowflies' magic and perseverance.

I saw the flash of his sharpening ivory fangs out of the corner of my eye. When I looked from the wound to his face, I wondered if I should be more frightened of him. He *was* a Kylorr, or at the very least, he had a lot of Kylorr blood in him. Their berserker natures were fearsome enough…but it was their bloodlust that had always given me greater pause.

He could drink me dry right here and right now, I thought, *and no one would know. No one would hear my screams in the Black Veil.*

A shudder raced down my spine, but I didn't move away. His pale blue eyes flickered over my face, settling on my lips…then the column of my neck.

The Kylorr and the Allavari were a strange blend, but they'd nearly always lived in this place together. For centuries, their blood had mixed.

But three hundred years ago, a strong hybrid male named Veranis Sarin had begun to practice a darker form of blood magic. His followers rose to power, practicing ancient sacrificial magic and spells that the Allavari had already banned for thousands of years. And so…unease spread throughout Allavar. Kylorr and Allavari hybrids were driven out from their villages, their homes. Hatred flowed through the valleys and fear tinged the air, so acrid one could choke on it.

Or so the stories went…

By all accounts, Veranis Sarin had been a power hungry and ambitious monster. He severed his soul—and those of his followers—from the living realm to open the portal to the Below. And the Allavari had banished them there.

Severs. The name of Veranis' followers, though innocent hybrids had been driven out with them, discriminated against for their mixed blood and nothing more.

Even now, though hybrids were commonplace in the villages once more, there were Allavari who gave them a wide berth, who whispered under their breath when they passed.

"I may have the antidote for night nettle," I said in a quiet rush. His gaze snapped up to mine and held. I saw his stomach dip, sucking in a sharp breath. I'd heard the pain from this particular poison was unfathomable. No wonder his pain had led me here, like a beacon in his dark forest. "But you'll need to come with me. Can you manage it?"

"Yes," he said. "Help me up."

I pushed to my feet quickly, rounding to his left side so I wouldn't jostle his wound. As I helped him to stand, he leaned into me heavily. I'd forgotten how large he was. I was tall for a human, and even then, he towered over me. His body was leanly muscled like an Allavari hunter, but I knew the Kylorr could morph into hulking beasts, given the proper stimulation. His wings hung limp, the ends dragging on the forest floor as I led him forward.

Heal him first...then ask questions, I thought. Night nettle wasn't a common poison. It was used only by certain individuals on Allavar, individuals who most knew to steer clear from. Even if one could afford the raw ingredients, it still needed to be extracted and prepared by a practiced hand, the process taking weeks.

If someone poisoned you with night nettle...they *wanted*—or needed—you dead.

There was a building dread in my belly which told me what I thought I already knew. That I didn't *have* the antidote, that I'd sold my last vial to a dark-eyed Ernitian who'd offered me a price I couldn't refuse at the last market day.

The Kylorr was huffing, his breathing labored, as we trudged closer and closer to my cottage. But it was slow going. His legs seemed like they were heavy and the Black Veil didn't make our path easy.

Every sound made my head whip to the side. Every branch blowing in the breeze or skittering of an animal's retreat held me on edge. Whoever had done this…they couldn't be that far away. Were they watching us, even now?

A chill went down the back of my neck, just as I felt the Kylorr's muscles bunch tight against my arm, where I had it wrapped underneath his wings.

Glowing white eyes were watching us. A tall, winged figure, shadowed underneath the canopy of a nearby tree. *A Sever?* It would be the closest I'd ever been to one.

They had sharp horns like Kylorr, but they were tall like the Allavari. A black cloak billowed out from its large body. I couldn't make out its features, but those eyes were eerie and they watched us steadily, spurring me to pick up my pace.

"Ignore him," the Kylorr grated to me, making me shoot him a sharp, incredulous look even as my heart raced. "Don't even look at him, little witch."

The Sever followed us to my cottage, always staying in the darkness, never stepping foot into the moonlight. When we finally jolted over the protection spell, the safe boundary of my property, I felt like I could finally breathe.

My glowflies were quiet, the hush ominous. When we finally made it inside my cottage, I shouldered the door closed, scrambling with the lock, before the male stumbled over to a chair at my dining table. His body was laughable large for the chair, but I was concerned when I saw the sheen of sweat covering his forehead and the dulled, ashen pallor of his usually luminous skin.

Taking a deep, steadying breath to calm my shaking hands, I hurried to my storage shelves lining the left wall next to my cauldron. Pulling open drawer after drawer, my eyes sought out the familiar cerulean vial of the brightbell-infused antidote. Every drawer ratcheted up my anxiety and the abysmal sense of failure.

"You don't have it," he commented, almost nonchalantly, behind my turned back. "Fuck."

Fuck, indeed, I thought. *Think, Marion. There's always a way…*

Brightbell. What properties made it an antidote for night nettle?

It thickened the blood, slowing down the night nettle in the veins. And in Kylorr…

A jolt of a realization spurred me into motion, and I snagged carrowroot extract, a bottle of keeper's bone, and dried wrathweed from last season's harvest. It wouldn't be perfect…but it would be *something*. I couldn't sit and watch him die. No healer who had taken the oath, bound in blood and magic, would be able to do that.

I didn't have time to extract the marrow from the keeper's bone, so I snagged a sizeable piece out of the jar and handed it over.

"Bite through this," I ordered him. "Get to the marrow. Quickly."

Luckily he didn't question me, and I turned my back on him, hearing his fangs crunch through bone. I dumped wrathweed into my mortar, grinding it down with practiced motions of my pestle before mixing it with the carrowroot extract, the liquid sizzling on contact with the fine dust. My eyes watered at the pungent smell, nausea rising in my belly.

I thickened it into a paste, thick enough that it clung to the stone pestle. Then I scurried out to the garden, not looking once into the forest to see if the Sever was still lingering nearby. I went to the wrathweed bed, to the tiny little grave I'd pressed the glowfly into earlier in the night. Rich soil stuck to its body when I unearthed it. I didn't have time to dry it out.

"I'm sorry, little one," I whispered, "but you just might save a life tonight."

A life for a life. Maybe there was a reason why this glowfly had died tonight of all nights.

Keeping the cold glowfly cupped in my palm, I returned to the cottage, catching movement out of the corner of my eye. The

Sever was still there. Strangely enough, his white eyes weren't on me. They were on my garden.

Bolting the door once more, I returned to my mortar, dropping the glowfly's lifeless body into the mix, soil and all. When I ground him into the paste, his blood shimmered blue, a dark dye against the sickening gray mixture.

Turning toward the male—whose name I didn't even know but had imagined a thousand different ways—I set my mortar on the table, eyeing the arrow.

"You're going to hate me for this," I informed him, keeping my voice low and steady.

His jaw tightened. There was understanding in his gaze. He knew the arrow needed to come out.

"Do it," he said. "I've had worse, I assure you."

His lips even quirked up in a half smile, and I nearly believed him.

I didn't know if he was lying or not—but I couldn't imagine anything worse than an arrow covered in night nettle poison. His face was leeched of any color it had previously possessed. He looked on the verge of passing out, his wings limp around him, slumped as he was in the chair. He'd spit out the husk of the bone onto the floor, but at least the marrow would help clot his blood.

I grabbed my strongest shears. He groaned, low in his throat, when I secured them against the shaft of the arrow, jostling the wound when it clamped down. I snapped the wood, splintering it as the male flinched and the fletching dropped to the floor. It made a bright *clink* when it hit, and I frowned when I realized it was *metal*.

"What's your name?" I asked him.

"Trying to distract me, little witch?" he pondered, his words a little slurred.

"My name is Marion, not *little witch*," I told him, sweat beginning to bead on my brow, and I shoved a wavy clump of my auburn hair away when it escaped from my braid. "Lean forward."

The Kylorr's leather vest creaked quietly when he did as I ordered. By some small miracle, the arrow had gone cleanly through, the arrowhead—also metal, I noted—poking out the back of his shoulder. I took my forceps, hooking them beneath the points.

"Your name," I prompted…before I gave one mighty, swift tug—not hesitating because hesitation would only make it hurt more. The shaft was smooth, a great mercy. I'd seen barbed ones before.

The Kylorr bellowed, loud and hoarse, and I dropped the arrow, rinsing the wound with clean water before taking up my mortar.

"Face of an angel…soul of a demon wanting vengeance," he told me, his gaze fastening with mine, though his eyes were half-lidded. "That's what the villagers say about you, Marion."

I froze, the words spearing me straight through me like I had taken a poisoned arrow of my own. I didn't think he'd meant to say them. He was half-delirious from night nettle.

"I'm trying to save your life, Kylorr," I replied calmly, as if my throat wasn't tightening. I blinked back the sting of tears. Even after all this time, the villagers still whispered behind my back. I didn't know if they would ever accept me, the strange human who lived in the Black Veil.

"Lorik," he rasped. "Lorik Ravael."

I began to pack the wound with the thick paste.

Lorik Ravael. After all these months, I finally knew his name.

That name proved what I'd already suspected. He was a Kylorr…but he was also Allavari.

I'd watched this male at the market before. *Everyone* watched him. He had an undeniable magnetism, an unparalleled draw that few ever possessed, that few might ever experience. If I didn't know better, I'd say it was magic.

"I don't have the soul of a demon, Lorik Ravael," I informed him.

His mouth widened, showing teeth—razor-sharp teeth that made me breath hitch. "Never said you did, Marion."

I continued packing the seeping wound, but the keeper's bone marrow was doing well to stop the bleeding.

Lorik hissed, his eyes closing briefly when I put pressure on his shoulder. I was hesitant about what would come next...but I didn't see a way around it.

Shoving my wrist in front of his face, I ordered softly, "Feed."

Lorik's eyes flashed open. "No," he grated, the word surprisingly harsh and quick.

"Yes," I said, my tone edging toward impatience. "After all this work, I'll be very annoyed if you die on me. The keeper's bone will thicken your blood. And luckily for you, Kylorr, you metabolize blood faster than most. But you still need *more* to help cleanse the poison from you."

"It's not me I'm worried about," Lorik said, making me frown.

"Even this might not save you," I snapped. The words were harsh but honest. It hadn't worked for Aysia, after all. "You're wasting time. *Feed.*"

As if to entice him, I pressed my inner wrist to his lips, surprisingly soft and warm.

Lorik met my eyes. Pale blue and luminous, like the wrathweed glowflies.

"Very well, little witch," came his strained, whispered words across my delicate flesh.

It happened quickly. His fangs flashed, elongating swiftly, twice in size what they had been. He bit down, greed and hunger evident in his eyes.

The pain was fleeting, giving way to something entirely unexpected as his venom flooded into my bloodstream.

My eyes widened, my knees nearly giving way with surprise.

Pleasure warmed me, flowing up my wrist into my throat, my chest, my belly. Down and down, it burst in me, pooling between my thighs, making me gasp.

Lorik groaned as my blood hit him, but I didn't think it was from pain.

No, no, no, I thought wildly. *What have I done?*

I might've just stepped unknowingly into the crosshairs of fate.

CHAPTER 3

There was a half-naked and slumbering Kylorr-Allavari in my bed, the first male to ever lie within its comfortable confines.

And he was held teetering on the edge of death.

He was sweating out the poison—as he had been since midnight—and if he survived that, the infection would take hold next.

But Lorik Ravael was strong. His heart had beat steadily and proudly beneath my cool palm when I'd checked it last. The night nettle was gifting him strange nightmares, and I watched from the doorway as he moaned and thrashed, his wings twitching underneath him. His shoulder was bandaged, but I'd left the wound open for now. It needed regular cleanings, and I needed to keep it packed with fresh poultice every few hours before I stitched it.

My forearm was beginning to burn from grinding the dried wrathweed in the early morning hours, but it needed to be done. Beneath the clean, white bandage, the bite on my wrist throbbed.

Heal him first...ask questions later, I reminded myself.

But I knew from my studies, from stories, from *history*...that a Kylorr's bite only triggered *that* kind of response in their mates. Their blood mates. *Kyranas*—that was what they called them in their language. Their venom reacting with their mate's blood, creating an overwhelming cacophony of sensation, meant to bond and tether the pairing together. Often for *life*.

That was what history said. *History*. *Kyrana* pairings…I'd never heard of one on Allavar. Not for centuries, at least. They happened commonly on Krynn, the Kylorr's home planet, because of their deities, because of the magic that infused that world.

But Allavar was different. The rules were different. The magic here was not the same.

I exhaled a slow breath and turned from the doorway. Looking at his face made my chest ache, as it always had. I'd be lying if I said I hadn't fantasized about Lorik in my bed before, though I hadn't known his name then. I'd be lying if I said I hadn't touched myself to the memory of his teasing grin and mischievous eyes, if I hadn't fantasized about those wings wrapping around me as he—

"Enough, Marion," I whispered, my cheeks flushing. This was improper. Having these thoughts about a half-dead, half-naked, half-Kylorr, half-Allavari male, who'd always sent a shiver down my spine. Was I intrigued? Yes. But that shiver also told me he was dangerous. There was something I couldn't see with Lorik. Something beneath the surface that had always sent a sharp warning spearing through my belly.

And others sense it too, I thought, remembering how most villagers gave him a wide berth at the market.

I thought that, perhaps, it was because of his mixed race. Allavari magic manifesting in a Kylorr? That was an extremely dangerous and powerful thing. Veranis Sarin—or his followers—wouldn't have been so powerful without his mixed blood, after all. And while the centuries had softened the fear of that in the villagers, it wasn't gone. There was a reason why people still looked at Kylorr-and-Allavari couples with a lingering, disapproving stare.

Lorik was a mystery I knew better than to investigate too deeply. Even as I acknowledged that, my eyes strayed to the floor in the front room, to the bloodied remnants of the arrow that had been protruding from his chest.

Reaching down, I gathered up the broken pieces as sunlight peeked through the shutters of my windows. I turned the fletching and the arrowhead in my fingers. Silver metal. But Allavari—though renowned and talented metallurgists in all the Four Quadrants—didn't use metal in arrows. They thought it a waste of their precious resources. Not even Allavari hunters used arrows anymore.

Sighing, I dropped the tips into an empty bowl to wash and snagged a fresh rag to clean up the memory of midnight. I heard a soft warbling, husky sound behind me and turned to see Peek emerging from beneath the kitchen counters.

"There you are," I murmured. "That's where you've been this whole time, you little coward?"

He mewed in answer, and I shook my head, reaching out to scratch behind his ears that were nearly as long as his body.

"We have a guest," I told Peek. "So, be nice."

My *braydus*'s eyes narrowed. Then he turned his head to regard the open doorway of my bedroom, his back hunching in response. In a flash, he leaped to the cottage door, pawing at it, and I let him out into the front garden.

Turning my face up to the sun, I soaked in the warm rays, even as the chilly air made me tighten my shawl around my shoulders. I was certain I looked like a mess. My nightdress was covered in black blood. Wrist bandaged. Braid askew. Deep circles under my eyes.

I smiled. The sun felt like *life*.

That was what Aysia always used to say. She'd woken early in the mornings to catch every last ray. At the orphanage,

Correl had been hard pressed to get her back inside most days…likely why my sister's back and legs had been covered in welts. Likely why I'd done everything I could to learn how to heal her quickly, to make her feel better so she wouldn't cry at night.

Grief and guilt and memory made my smile fade. The sun's warmth turned oppressive, and I retreated back into my cottage but left the door open to help air out the stink of the poultice and the fire cups still simmering in the hearth.

"Aysia, you silly lovesick darling," I murmured to myself, missing her. Some days, it felt like an open wound, one that would never heal.

"Do you often talk to yourself, little witch?" came his voice, tired and rumbled. "Or is that the madness of the Black Veil manifesting in you?"

A little embarrassed he'd caught me, I turned slowly and said, "You should be in bed still."

The left corner of his full mouth twitched up. "You're not the first female to say that to me."

He looked to be in a sorry state. Hunched over, skin shimmering with sweat, damp hair sticking to his, admittedly, impressively well-defined chest. He *was* a Kylorr, after all.

Leaning heavily against the doorframe of my bedroom, Lorik ran his gaze over me. His eyes settled on the bandage over my wrist, and I felt his eyes burn there like a brand. The bite throbbed, the mortifying memory of temporary insanity rising.

My face felt hot. My legs felt like they were suddenly made of stone.

He'd fed from me greedily. Roughly, even. As if he couldn't get enough of my blood. And in return, I'd nearly come apart at my seams, moaning out my disbelief, before I couldn't take it anymore. I'd ripped myself away, tearing the skin, making myself bleed even more.

"You didn't let me heal you last night," Lorik said. I felt the richness of his voice thread and weave into my body. "I don't remember what came afterward. But I do remember that."

He made the room feel entirely too small, even though he kept a respectable distance and he looked like a wind gust could blow him over.

There was a strain in his eyes that hadn't been there before. I wondered what the nightmares had been.

"I'm serious, Lorik," I said quietly. "You need to be resting."

The mysterious male stared at me across the room, neither of us making a move.

"Why did you save me?"

My brow furrowed. "What do you mean?"

"You woke in the middle of the night, ventured out into the Black Veil, and risked your safety to help me. Why?" Lorik asked. "For all you know, I could be a danger to you too."

Heart picking up speed, I asked, "Are you? A danger to me?"

Lorik didn't reply, only lowered his sharp chin slightly. Was that an affirmative? Or because his head was growing heavy from weariness?

Much to my dismay, Lorik didn't return to bed. He shuffled over to the chair at the table he'd been sitting in the night before, freshly cleaned of his blood though I could still smell it in the air.

"Why?" I repeated. "Because I'm a healer. It's my duty. The oath I took under Allavari law."

"And bound in their magic?" he wondered.

I inclined my head. "Yes."

"Ah, so you see," he said softly, whistling. "If you didn't help me, knowing I needed it, you would be punished. You would feel pain if you yourself did not try to assuage it for another. Would you consider yourself a selfish person, little witch?"

I blinked, my spine straightening. Irritation rose in my chest, but I kept my face smooth. "No."

"Liar," he said, smiling though it looked more like a grimace on his face with the amount of discomfort he must've been in.

"I think we're all selfish. It's in every being's nature, in all the Four Quadrants, to look out for themselves and only themselves."

"And what about family? The ones you love?" I pondered, thinking of Aysia, *knowing* Lorik was wrong. "Are you telling me you wouldn't do anything in your power, even in the face of death, to help them?"

Lorik's lips lifted and he dropped his gaze to the floor. In agreement?

"Perhaps," I said, "I don't share your pessimism."

Lorik's sudden laugh jolted me, a booming, surprising sound. He laughed too loudly, too fully. My brows furrowed listening to it, watching him, even as my shoulders relaxed, liking the sound entirely too much.

"Oh, fuck, that hurts," he wheezed, his voice husky and strained but no less pleasing to my ears.

Peek's warbling mew sounded from the doorway, drawn in from the commotion. Lorik's head whipped over his shoulder, likely tugging on the wound, and I frowned, my lips parting to order him back to bed. He needed to keep his heartbeat steady, and he certainly didn't need to be stretching his wound.

"A *braydus*?" Lorik said, voice wistful. "Wherever did you find it?"

My soft spot was Peek, however, as I enjoyed talking about him and hardly ever got the chance to. I found myself straying to the front doorway of my cottage, Lorik turning in his chair to regard me. I scooped up Peek, his long, soft fur tickling my arms and brushing over the bandaged bite on my wrist, the press of his body making it throb.

"In the forest," I told Lorik. "Years ago now. He was only just born and I looked for days for the mother but couldn't find her."

He was staring at Peek, a strange expression on his face.

"What is it?" I asked, trying to relax the stiff *braydus* in my arms as the two regarded one another.

"The *braydus* come from the Below," Lorik murmured. "Aren't you worried its magic will draw Severs?"

"What are you talking about?" I questioned. "There are *braydus* all over these woods. They didn't come from the Below."

Lorik's gaze flashed up to mine. "That's a pure *braydus* you have in your arms. You can tell by the eyes."

I looked down at Peek, his vibrant blue orbs shimmering in the sunlight.

"It came from the Below. I'm only surprised you don't have Severs at your door nightly wanting it back," Lorik said.

"His name is Peek," I informed him, my tone testy, glancing back up at the mysterious male across from me, whose lips quirked. "And I don't. I have a protection barrier placed around my property every moon cycle."

"And you think that keeps Severs away?" Lorik questioned, his tone agonizingly smug for someone the color of dampened ash. "An Allavari witch's spell is no match for a Sever. Surely you know that."

"Well, it's worked. For years," I snapped, my shoulders going back as I let Peek back down to the floor when he began to struggle. "The Severs stay beyond the property line. Not once have they ever been able to step foot toward the cottage."

Lorik's eyes narrowed and his gaze dropped back to Peek, who regarded him with a hunched back from the floor, hiding behind my legs.

"Then that is your *braydus*'s magic, not that of an Allavari witch. You have yourself a protector," Lorik said, his tone decided. "Lucky for you, it is *Peek* who keeps the Severs away."

I laughed. "I think the infection has taken root. Do you feel feverish?"

"Don't believe me?" he questioned, leaning heavily in the chair. His bared chest *was* shimmering with sweat.

"The *braydus* live in the Black Veil, and they have for centuries. They certainly have no magic. Peek's only ability is to eat far more than he should, and he is particularly gifted at catching poor rodents and leaving them on the doorstep. But he certainly didn't come from *the Below*"—even thinking it was laughable—"and he doesn't keep Severs away. A very pricey monthly spell does."

Lorik's eyes began to glitter, but I thought it was a trick of the light. When I blinked, they returned to their blue state.

"Are you often driven by logic and intellect, Marion?" Lorik asked. "Or do you think there may be a chance that there are things in this universe even you cannot understand or expect? Things that might challenge the way you think and upheave every last thing you think you know?"

"*Logically*, I know there are *many* things in this universe I cannot begin to understand."

Lorik laughed again, this time softer, and Peek crept closer to him, sniffing the air.

"You are a peculiar woman," he said, watching my *braydus* approach him. "And if we were on Krynn, perhaps, why might you think fate chose you for me?"

I stiffened, my face going hot. The first mention to *what* I suspected. He knew it too.

Damn.

"What does your logic decide about *that*?" Lorik wanted to know, that smug smirk appearing on his face, making the room appear entirely too small again.

"That…that was a fluke," I told him, straightening my spine, my eyes dropping to Peek as he sniffed Lorik's boots, which I hadn't taken off him after I'd lugged him to bed. Peek hissed and backed away slowly. "It's possible the keeper's bone had some sort of adverse reaction. Your fangs were coated in it, so when you bit down—"

"Shall we put it to the test again? The scientist in you would appreciate that, surely."

The flush seemed to spread from my cheeks to just about everywhere else.

"That won't be necessary," I huffed. "You need to go back to bed now. You're…you're upsetting Peek."

Lorik's slow gaze dropped to my *braydus* and then slowly came back to meet mine. "Right. Peek. Wouldn't want that, would we, little witch?"

He stood and returned to the bedroom. When he was out of sight, I sagged against the wall, blowing out a long, silent breath.

Lorik Ravael needed to heal…and then he needed to leave. The sooner, the better.

Before this thread between us strengthened until neither of us could untangle ourselves from it.

CHAPTER 4

Lorik didn't wake again until nightfall. He found me out in the garden, tending to my glowflies.

I didn't sense his presence until Peek came sauntering out from the Black Veil and then immediately hissed, his eyes pinned on something behind me. Thinking it was a Sever, I stiffened...until I looked over my shoulder and found Lorik regarding me from the stone bench wedged against the back wall of my cottage.

"How long have you been there?" I asked, surprised, straightening from the garden bed, my arms covered in rich, black soil as a shadevine glowfly nearly got tangled in my wavy hair. I shook him out, getting his dust in my strands, making them gleam. Had he heard me singing to myself?

"Long enough," Lorik grunted. He was hunched slightly, his wings looking uncomfortably squished against the wall of my home. He looked tired, dark circles under his eyes, though he'd slept the day away. "You're horribly unobservant. I've decided you must have had Severs come onto your land—you just haven't noticed them."

"So you admit that Peek isn't from the Below and *doesn't* have magic that keeps Severs away?"

Lorik grumbled something under his breath, in a language that sounded familiar but new, and I grinned.

Being out in my garden always lightened my mood. The dust from the glowflies possessed calming qualities and their buzzing lulled me into a gentle trance, but it was the gardening I enjoyed the most. Tending to the plants my glowflies were growing, weeding, snipping away weak leaves that would only take more energy to heal, watering where needed.

"You're different out here," Lorik remarked. "*This* is you, little witch. In your garden where you sing, where you are free."

The grin died from my face, even though his words filled me with a strange, fluttering warmth.

"You have a beautiful voice," he complimented. "You were singing an Allavari poem, weren't you?"

The Allavari poem Aysia had always liked. I'd often sing it at night at Correl's home for the other children as they'd drifted off to sleep. I'd been the oldest there. I would tuck them all into their beds at night, and they would always want a song or a story.

The poem was about love…on its surface. That had been Aysia's favorite part. But the last verse was a dark warning, for the Allavari girl's lover consumed her heart like a feasting Sever, though Aysia had always thought it was interpreted as the girl giving her heart away. *Romantic,* she'd sighed, and I'd always bitten my tongue, not wanting to disappoint her.

Perhaps I should have, I couldn't help but think, a prick of guilt making me stand from my kneeling position. I journeyed to the garden bed closest to Lorik, kneeling down at its side as I began to pluck away fallen leaves from the trees overhead that littered the soil.

"Severs don't feast on hearts though," Lorik said quietly, watching me work. "Not anymore, at least."

"How are you feeling?" I asked, ignoring what he'd said.

"Like death itself," he replied, though he grinned, his fangs flashing in the moonlight, making my breath hitch.

Deep down, I knew he would need to feed again and soon. I was dragging my feet, however, not wanting the confirmation of what I already feared.

Another day, I thought. Surely he could go another day. I would feed him a hearty bone broth tonight to nourish him, and then he could feed on blood tomorrow.

"You were on the brink of it," I told him, feeling a tightening in my chest at the thought. I didn't know if he understood how dangerous night nettle poison was.

"I'm stronger than I look, Marion."

There was something in his voice, a muted confidence that had nothing to do with bravado and everything to do with *fact*, that reassured me he was telling the truth.

And the way he said my name made a warm shiver stroke down my spine.

"Who shot you with the arrow?" I asked, the question I'd been pondering since I'd found him last night finally out in the open between us.

"Perhaps I did it to myself so that a beautiful human witch would take pity on me and allow me to warm her bed," he said, "when I have been dreaming of it for so long."

His words brought a dizzying rush of heat to my belly.

"The arrow tip pierced all the way through your shoulder. Even with your strength as a Kylorr, even if you somehow were in your berserker state—which you weren't—you would've needed a bow for that. Quite impossible to shoot yourself," I pointed out, if only to distract from the rapid beating of my heart.

"Is that what your beloved logic tells you?" he asked. I'd looked down to the brightbell plant I was tending to—ironically, the plant that would have been the antidote to the night nettle poison had it been fully grown—but I heard the smile in his voice.

I shrugged a shoulder.

He chuffed out a small sigh. When I looked back at him, he had his face tipped back to the night sky, his eyes closed. I paused in plucking out leaves to watch him. My gaze drifted down the long, thick column of his throat, over his shoulders, one of them tightly wound in clean gauze, down the slabs of muscles lining his chest.

"Who do you think shot me with an arrow?" he asked.

"There is an Allavari who lives in the village," I said quietly. Swallowing down my hatred and bitterness, I said, "His name is Veras."

Lorik laughed, but there was an edge to it. "You think that useless piece of flesh managed to shoot me with a poisoned arrow?"

I frowned. "If he heard you speaking about him like that, he surely would. He's a dangerous male. You should be more careful with your tongue."

"I welcome him to try," Lorik rumbled. "It would give me a reason to tear him limb from limb."

I nearly shuddered at the bloodlust in his voice…and yet…

"You like it when I'm bloodthirsty, little witch?" he teased, his voice morphing into velvety softness. "You *hate* Veras. Would you like me to give you his still-beating heart? Perhaps that can be my repayment to you. For saving my life, I will give you his. I will give you one favor, Marion, and it can be whatever you want. I vow I will grant it."

I couldn't tell him just how much I was tempted to say yes—because there was an instinct in me that told me Lorik *meant it*. That this male was much, much more dangerous than Veras could ever hope to be, even with his henchmen carrying out his bidding and his manipulative pull within the village.

"Don't," I said quietly. "I am a healer, not an accomplice."

"Even after what he did to your sister?"

I couldn't contain my sharp breath. It was no secret. Lorik

had obviously asked about me throughout the village—and I didn't know how I felt about *that*.

"I would do anything for my sister—you were right earlier," Lorik said, his tone turning savage and I leveled him a sharp look. "I imagine you would've too."

"Then you're not so selfish as you insisted," I pointed out, filing away the fact that he had a sister, one I'd never seen. Did she live in the village? Where did *Lorik* even live?

"Did I say that?" he asked, his mood unreadable.

"You implied it." And he knew it too.

Lorik stared at me, and then his mouth slowly drew into a grin, his teeth appearing even sharper in the moonlight. For the first time, I had the instinct to run from him. Warning bells in my mind battled with the warmth in my chest.

"A Sever shot me with the arrow."

I jolted, gasping. "What?"

I always felt out of control with him. Even when I'd met him at the market all those months ago. He'd always made me feel like I was walking on trembling ground.

It was unsettling. *Exciting*. Unpredictable.

Unless he's lying, I thought.

"But…but *why?*"

"How should I know?" Lorik asked, holding my gaze, his blue eyes glittering again in the silver light.

"So a *Sever* just…came up from the Below, tracked you down in the Black Veil in the middle of the night where you happened to be, and shot you with a poisoned, metal-tipped arrow they just happened to have prepared?"

"It would appear so," he said.

He's lying, I thought. Of course he was. That story was ridiculous. Severs hunted with their claws and fangs like wild beasts. Not with a bow. It still didn't explain what Lorik *had* been doing in the Black Veil at midnight.

"Whatever it is that you're involved in," I started quietly, "don't pull me into it. I helped you. I saved your life. I don't need your problems spilling into mine. Veras already took the one person I loved most in this world. And if you're involved with him, in any way, I need to know. Right now."

Lorik held my gaze, his features sobering for a brief moment.

"I'm not involved with Veras, Marion," Lorik told me, his voice gruff and soft. "Not now, not ever."

My shoulders relaxed. Maybe I was a fool, but I heard truth in his voice.

"Does that mean you'll let me stay in your bed?" he asked, the question helping to ease some of the tension that had risen between us.

I tried to hide the way my lips quirked.

"Just until you heal," I told him. "And I'm convinced you're free of infection."

"Perhaps you'll even join me there tonight," he rasped. "I'll keep you warm with my infected, feverish body."

The laugh that bubbled up my throat…that one I couldn't help.

All the amusement left Lorik's face, and he stared at me until my laugh slowly died, until I pushed a strand of hair behind my ear, grazing my cheek with soil.

"What is it?"

"You have a beautiful laugh too," Lorik said. But gone was the teasing lilt in his voice. The words were guttural and raw and *honest*. An honest compliment, devoid of any expectation. I didn't know if *anyone* had ever spoken to me like that before.

"Oh," I whispered, pleased, embarrassed. "Thank you."

"Will you sing again for me?" he asked, settling more fully against the wall, though I was concerned about the growing chill in the air and the sweat slicking his chest. He paused. "Though maybe not that poem. I'm not fond of tragic endings."

I studied this half-Kylorr, half-Allavari male, wondering

where in the world he had come from. I suddenly wanted to know *everything*.

"All right," I said, thinking that with those glittering blue eyes, he could ask me to go to the Below itself and I would.

And so I sang for him. I sang as I tended to my garden, as the moon slowly rose, as my glowflies buzzed all around me, and as Peek even settled close by without hissing at our guest once.

All the while, Lorik never took his eyes off me.

CHAPTER 5

Lorik hid his infection well. Better than most…until it reared its head the following night.

And it was ugly. The ugliest I'd ever seen.

"You stupid fool," I whispered without malice, stroking a cloth I intermittently dipped in cold water across his face and down his chest.

Earlier this afternoon, he'd been burning up, his flesh nearly scorching to the touch. The only ray of hope had been the night nettle weeping out from his skin, a blue cast staining the washcloth, and requiring me to use gloves to touch him.

But there was no evidence of the poison now as he lay in my bed, thrashing restlessly in his deep sleep, his chest heaving. His long, dark hair was tangled around his sharp horns, and I'd nearly gouged my wrist trying to untangle it, so I left it be.

My back was beginning to ache from the chair I'd been situated in for nearly the entire day. I thought of how lucid and present he'd been last night, sitting in the back garden with me for seemingly hours until the chill had turned bitter.

I sang as I wiped his brow. Old Allavari songs, coupled with some human ones, ancient tales of our home planet, of Earth.

I had a few wax candles lit, infused with lovery leaves, the gentle smoke filling the air to help him breathe more easily. Shadows flickered over his sharp features, and I studied every dip and line and angle, trying to separate the Allavari from the Kylorr and failing.

There was something incredibly…*other* about him. I couldn't place why.

"What is that song?" he murmured quietly without opening his eyes.

I kept my hand steady, pressing the cold cloth to his neck, though relief flowed heavy in my veins.

"A human song," I murmured, watching his eyes flicker open.

Not a trick of the light, I thought, studying his eyes. They *were* glittering blue, the colors shifting in his irises, and my heart began to pick up pace in my chest.

"You know their old language? *Your* old language?" he corrected, his voice paper thin but no less pleasing.

"No," I admitted, swallowing, averting my eyes from his to focus on the cloth. "I'm sure I'm jumbling the words, but I memorized how they sounded. When I was…when I was at the orphanage, Correl had an old Halo orb. I found it in the cellar and repaired it so we could access the Quadrants' databases. And we would play music at night, from all over the universe. The children always wanted to hear Allavari lullabies or Ernitian ballads. I was one of the only humans there, so I listened to my ancestors' songs after they fell asleep."

Lorik listened to me speak, his chest heaving with his labored breaths.

"It sounds beautiful," he told me. "It sounds like you know the words, that you truly feel them when you sing."

"Sometimes I wonder if we instinctively know our ancient languages. Like the words still speak to some part of me," I told him, my lips curling in a small smile.

"It's a nice sentiment."

I nodded, chancing a peek back up at his glittering eyes, wondering if I should be afraid of them.

"Very few races now live on their home planets. Language is forever changed because of it," I said. "Especially the universal language…that's the only one I know. It's evolved and changed over centuries. And though it's universal, it's different everywhere but similar enough to communicate at the travel ports. Our language on Allavar? It's the universal tongue, yes, but it's also littered with old Allavari and even Kylorr languages. Ernitians have a difficult time with it, I know, when they first come here."

"Were you born in the village?" he wondered. "In Rolara?"

"Yes," I told him. "It's the only place I've known. Were you?"

He closed his eyes briefly. "No. Not in the village."

"But on Allavar?" I prompted.

"Yes."

"So secretive," I teased gently, watching his eyelids lift and a familiar expression take over his features, though it was tired. I studied the ever-changing blue of his eyes. "Keep your secrets, Lorik. I'm not sure I want to know them."

"And what secrets do you have, I wonder?" Lorik asked, his voice a soft rasp, drifting over my skin.

That I'm afraid, I thought immediately. *So very afraid. Of dying alone in the Black Veil, of never knowing true love, of never having a family of my own, of having crushing regrets as I take my last breath.*

"I have nothing to hide," I told him. "I live a quiet life, and there's no reason to keep secrets."

"Everyone has secrets," he told me. "One of yours for one of mine."

I let out a gentle laugh.

"It can be anything," he added, sounding tired.

"Don't you think I deserve all your secrets after tending to you all day?" I asked. "I've seen you at your worst. What else can you be hiding?"

35

Something flashed over his face, a surprisingly intense expression, especially when he still looked like he was on the threshold of death's door.

"But I'll play along," I told him, if only to keep talking to him. I didn't want to admit how worried I'd been today. He hadn't woken once. This was the first time since last night.

"I'm waiting," he prompted after a lengthy silence.

"I'm thinking."

"It takes you that long to think up a secret?"

One that I can tell you, yes, I thought silently. It was actually strangely difficult.

"Have you ever stolen anything?" he asked, trying to help.

"Yes!" I said, more excitedly than I probably should've, and his unexpected laugh made his chest heave. "Sorry. Yes, I have."

"And? What did you steal, little witch?"

I dipped the cloth back into the water in the basin before wringing it out.

"A bracelet," I told him. "My sister, Aysia, always looked at this one bracelet at a shop in the village. It's not there anymore, but back then, they had beautiful jewelry. Expensive. The owner, Merec, was a talented jeweler who imported gems from the northern islands, and he'd always smile at us when he saw us looking in the window."

Guilt rose, as it always did. Though, I often thought of Merec fondly, I didn't like to think of why we'd met.

"I knew him," Lorik said. "He was a friend of my father's. Long ago."

I filed that information away and continued, "The Lunaer Celebration was coming up, and I had no gift for her. It was her tenth year, and I wanted the gift to be special. And all I could think of was the bracelet. So one day, I went into the shop and when Merec had his back turned, I took it."

Lorik looked at me steadily, and I couldn't help but give him a half smile.

"I think my sister wanted the bracelet enough to not ask too many questions. She liked pretty things. But I couldn't sleep at night. I felt so guilty, taking something from someone who had only ever shown us kindness. So two days later, I went back to Merec and confessed what I'd done."

"And?"

I smoothed the cloth down Lorik's chest and felt it rumble with the spoken word. I could feel his heart beating beneath my palm, heat radiating off him, though he'd cooled significantly from earlier that afternoon.

"He told me to keep the bracelet, to let my sister have it, but that I needed to work in his shop to repay him," I said. "For three months I worked there, sneaking away from the home when I could. But it was the favorite part of my day. I enjoyed the tidying, the stocking, hearing the little bell ring when the door opened. It was so bright in there, the sunlight came streaming in through the windows, so I made sure they were clean every day. I grew to love the sound of drills and the rotation of the polishing basket. I always imagined hundreds of jewels tumbling in there."

I met Lorik's eyes. His legs were too long for my bed, but at least I'd taken off his boots this time. I'd needed to strip him down to nothing to fight the fever and only kept a sheet across his groin for privacy. But the outline of him was…distracting, and I felt guilty thinking that when he was ill and in my care.

"Then one day…I came to the shop and Merec was just *gone*. His jewelry was packed up. His tools cleared out. He left a note for me, short but nice, saying he was leaving Rolara but nothing more. He said he was glad we were friends. He left me some money—more money than I'd ever seen—which I used when I left Correl's. Without his generosity, I don't know what would have happened. And that was it. I never saw or heard from him again. But I think about him every time I walk past that shop. It's still empty. At one point, I thought I might take it over someday."

"Why don't you?" Lorik asked, shifting slightly in the bed, wings repositioning. He winced—the muscles, no doubt, stiff.

"You need money for that," I told him. "Besides, I do well enough on my potions, but...I could never leave my glowflies. The Black Veil is my home."

"Aren't you frightened of it?"

"You're asking for a lot of my secrets when you've given me none of yours," I pointed out.

Lorik trapped my wrist under his palm, and my breathing went tight. His coloring was lighter than the average Kylorr's, his skin a silvery tone of gray, making him appear like he was glowing...like he was otherworldly. Allavari had elf-like features and lithe, graceful silhouettes. With Lorik, it made for an interesting and overwhelming mix with the brute, winged strength of a powerful Kylorr male.

He was...magnetic. Beautiful but dangerous. I'd felt his pull long before now.

His finger stroked down my wrist, over the bandage there, and my heart sped.

"A secret?" he asked. A small smile played over his lips, despite the strain around his glittering blue eyes as they fixated on where he touched me. "I've thought about you far more than I should've these last few months, little witch."

I jerked, my tongue twisting, uncertain how to respond to that.

"But I need to give you a better secret than that after what you shared," he told me, his gaze flashing back up to mine. "What do you want to know?"

Too many questions to count, I couldn't help but think, my mind racing with possibility.

"Or perhaps I will tell you another's secret—would you like that?"

"Another's?" I asked, frowning. "Whose?"

"Merec's."

I stiffened, but Lorik never stopped stroking my wrist, the rough, flat pads of his fingertips journeying beyond the edge of the bandage.

"Merec left Rolara because he, like you, was indebted to someone. He left because it was time to repay it," Lorik told me.

"To who?" I asked, thinking what debt could possibly be so important that he'd packed up his entire life in a single night and left without a trace. People only did that when they were in trouble. Or scared. "Where did he go?"

Lorik inhaled a deep breath, smoothing his fingers down the inside of my arm, making tingles race up my spine.

"To the Below," he answered. "His debt was to a Sever."

CHAPTER 6

"*What?*" I whispered, wide-eyed. And I wasn't shocked or surprised by very much in this life. "A Sever?"

"There's your secret," Lorik told me. "No more this night."

"You can't just tell me that and say nothing else," I argued. "How do you know this?"

"Like I said, my father was good friends with Merec. *Is.*"

"So, he's…he's alive?"

"As far as I know," he murmured, closing his eyes again briefly.

"But it's the Below," I said, standing from the chair, my legs suddenly restless. Lorik's grip fell away from my wrist. He watched me as I paced, and I noticed that Peek was curled up near the door of my bedroom. Keeping an eye on our guest? "No one survives in the Below except Severs. It's impossible."

A flash of something crossed his expression. Annoyance? Disappointment?

"You know nothing about what is possible and what is not, Marion. Village folk shouldn't speak of something they know nothing about."

The sudden change in his mood had me quieting. His tone was stern. I felt like I was being scolded.

An uncomfortable silence dropped like a heavy stone between us.

Then he said, "I want to ask you something."

I studied him. Even lying back in the bed, half-poisoned, it felt like he still took up the majority of the room.

"Yes?" I asked.

"Are you the kind of person who believes what something *seems* that something *is*?"

"I don't understand," I admitted quietly.

He continued as if I hadn't spoken. "Or are you the kind of person who understands there are things that cannot be understood in this world, things that are not what they seem, and that if you understood them in their entirety, you would see that you understood nothing at all?"

"Do you often speak in riddles?" I wondered.

"There are two types of beings on Allavar," he murmured, his blue eyes glittering. Were they *glowing*? "Those who welcome change and those who don't, who resist it. Which one are you, little witch?"

"You tell me," I replied, stepping forward toward the bed. His eyes never left mine. "I left the safety of my home in the middle of the night to help a stranger, who is now sleeping in my bed. That's certainly a change."

"One might call that bravery," he said. "Or foolishness."

I jolted, annoyance beginning to build in my breast. I shot back, "Or duty."

Lorik's lips quirked tiredly, and he huffed out a sharp breath through his nostrils.

"From what I can see and from what I know, you've lived here a long time, since your sister's death, yes? All alone in the Black Veil, where most wouldn't even step foot. You tend to your glowflies and you keep your *braydus*, who you are certain never came from the Below. You go to the market every moon cycle to sell your potions and healing salves. You collect your money, and then you come back. To your cottage in the Black Veil. Alone. Where you tend to your glowflies and keep your *braydus*, who does in fact protect you more than you know."

I stood, frozen, looking down at him. My heart was pounding in my chest. Out of anger? Defensiveness? Or sadness? Loneliness?

"You don't know me at all" was all I could utter. And in the quiet of my room, it felt as pathetic as it sounded.

"Most would say you don't like change. You live a comfortable life. A peaceful one. But is it content? Are you happy?"

I didn't like to be criticized. And this? It felt like one big criticism of *my* life.

"Why do you even care?" I whispered harshly, glaring down at him. He wasn't fazed by my ire, however.

"Because I want to know everything about you, Marion."

My breath whooshed out of my lungs. Shock momentarily dispelled any displeasure I felt.

"I see a beautiful, empathetic, kind woman, who *did* leave the safety of her own home to help a stranger in the middle of the night. I see a woman who smiles at villagers in the market who don't even deserve it. I see a woman who has overcome struggle and tragedy but has still managed to build all of this. All by herself. Who sings like an Allavari angel and who has barely slept because she's been tending to a massive, nosy, irritating bastard who's disrupted her life. She would say it's her duty as a healer…but truthfully, I think it might be because she likes him too."

My cheeks felt warm.

"I want to understand that woman," Lorik said. "I want to know *you*. I have for some time."

My mind flashed to the first time we'd met. All those moon cycles ago in the market, on a drizzly, gray day. I remembered the way my heart had stopped at that mischievous, almost secretive grin when he'd stopped at my stall.

"You never...you never..."

"Asked your name? Asked you to the tavern for an Allavari ale after you packed up your wares? Flirted with you in one of the back booths there so I could steal your kiss and then another when I walked you home?"

"Well..." I trailed off, surprised, flustered. "*Yes.*"

"You didn't strike me as a woman who would welcome someone like me."

My brows furrowed. His tone was soft. Almost...somber. Quiet in its truth.

"You assume a lot, Lorik Ravael," I said, just as quietly. "Maybe instead of assuming, you could simply *ask*."

"Yes," Lorik said, his eyes closing for a brief moment. I thought I saw something shimmer over his skin, but when the candle's light flickered, I knew my eyes were just playing tricks on me. "You're right, little witch. So when I'm recovered and not sweating out poison in your bed, would you join me for an Allavari ale at Grimstone's Tavern?"

Despite the ache in my back from tending to him the better part of the day and the annoyance in my chest from his earlier words, a small laugh escaped me.

"You don't have to call it an Allavari ale, you know," I pointed out. "We are in Allavar. You just call it ale."

"Was that an answer?"

I tucked a stray strand of hair behind my ear, suddenly shy.

"Yes," I said. "Yes, I'll join you at Grimstone's."

Lorik's eyes shone. He went quiet, simply watching me, and I fidgeted under his gaze. Embarrassed but pleased with his slow perusal and observation.

"For the sake of honesty, Marion," he warned, his tone deep and husky, "I won't lie—I'll likely try to steal a kiss long before Grimstone's ever happens."

Excitement displaced my previous annoyance. This was new. It felt…dizzying. To be wanted. To be pursued. Especially by *him*.

"I might even let you," I rushed out.

The sound he made was a cross between a groan and a laugh.

Feeling flushed and uncertain, I said quickly, "You should rest now."

"You expect me to rest after that admission?" he wanted to know.

"Yes," I said, trying to regain some authority in my voice. He was still a patient of mine, after all. And though his fever had come down, he wasn't out of the woods yet.

I didn't understand it. Allavari were powerful. Kylorr too, in their own way, though they possessed no natural-born magic. He should have been able to overcome this. But he'd taken a turn for the worse today.

Something occurred to me, and I let out a small, shuddering sigh.

It had been over a day since he'd fed on my blood. Perhaps his body needed more to cleanse the remainder of the poison and fight the infection that had taken root.

Glancing down at my wrist, I eyed the bandage, before studying him.

"Are you…hungry?" I asked softly.

His blue eyes seemed to glow brighter. His jaw tightened.

"Why didn't you say something?" I asked.

"It's not that…" he said. "It's not that I am. I don't *need* blood. Like Kylorr, it's only a…a perk."

"You're sick. I'm sorry—I should have realized," I told him, unwrapping the bandage on my wrist. I heard him swallow hard. The edge of one of his wings twitched as I approached. "Let me help you sit up."

With my help, Lorik maneuvered upright so he leaned

against the wooden headboard of my bed. He took up nearly the entire thing.

There would be no room for me unless I was draped over him, came the stray thought.

"This…this is just a feeding," I said slowly, meeting his eyes. I remembered the warm pleasure that had taken hold before. I didn't know if I'd be able to look at another Kylorr's fangs the same again.

His lips quirked, no doubt trying to bring some lightness and levity to the tension strumming tightly between us. "Like my medicine?"

My grin felt too wide on my face, too flustered by the sudden pounding in my breast and the way the healing wound on my wrist began to throb.

"Yes, exactly," I told him, raising my wrist and sitting down. The pads of Lorik's fingers, the heat and caress of them, made me shiver when he took it. He brushed his thumb over the vein, and my breath hitched in anticipation.

Perched on the edge of my bed, I was close enough to him to see the sudden swirling in his eyes. Was that a common trait in Kylorr-Allavari?

Our gaze connected and held. This close, I could smell the sharpness of the night nettle, but underneath that, I smelled crushed silver leaves and willowroot moss—earthy but crisp.

He smelled like the Black Veil at dawn.

His fangs elongated. They ran over the vein he'd traced with his thumb.

Then he bit down.

CHAPTER 7

His choked groan made my eyes close as his venom flooded the bite.

At first it felt like I was floating. A pleasant buzz, a gentle lightness spreading through my limbs, down and up my spine, prickling my scalp, and making my legs twitch. My breathing got heavy, but I tried to keep still. I felt a tugging pull on my wrist, felt the suction on my flesh.

I bit my lip as warmth began to spread. Like an ink bottle spilling, the arousal pooled slowly, inching outward, little by little until I felt it cover me completely. It absorbed itself into my skin and then spilled between my thighs. Every pull at my wrist made it grow. Every tug made me swallow, and I bit my lip.

Perhaps it's for the best he's not a full-blooded Kylorr, I thought to myself, dazed, *that he has Allavari blood running in his veins.*

Kyranas, they'd called them. Long ago. A Kylorr's fated mate, tied to them by blood and pleasure. Every feeding brought ecstasy. But the days of *kyranas* for hybrids were long past, at least on Allavar. Once the Kylorr and Allavari blood had mixed, once the Severs had gone to the Below, there had been no reports of *kyranas*. They were growing rarer and rarer beyond Krynn's—the Kylorr's home planet—borders.

But in its place, there was *this*. A gentler version of what a *kyrana* feeding had been…only *these* were much more common, or so I'd heard. I'd been fed from once before, but that had been with Aysia…there had been nothing remotely sexual about it.

But *this*…

With Lorik, it was completely and utterly different.

He huffed out a sharp breath through his nostrils. The heat spread over my wrist, and I shifted in place on the bed. His back hunched even more, dragging me closer until he was gripping my shoulder with one hand, the other pressed into my forearm, holding me in place. As if afraid I'd back away.

Magic flowed over my sensitive skin. It prickled at my scalp, making me gasp. He was powerful, I realized. More so than I'd first thought. His Allavari magic was tangible—I'd never quite felt anything like it before.

I breathed in deeply, scenting the lovery leaves from the wax candle, heady and earthy. I let that scent ground me, keep me focused as Lorik fed.

I didn't know how long it went on. It felt both endless and quick. When Lorik dislodged his fangs from my wrist, he did so with a gruff groan, as if loath to leave me. Those blue eyes flashed up to mine, glowing more brightly than I'd seen.

"What are you?" I whispered, brow furrowing, voice sounding far away.

Lorik pressed his lips to my wound, making my own part in wanting. When he pulled away, the fang marks were gone. As if the feeding had never happened in the first place. Erased. Except I would never be able to forget it.

"You don't want to know, little witch," he replied.

When he let go of my wrist, I pulled away, standing from the bed. I tried to get hold of myself, going to the candle burning on the side table, scraping a piece of wax with the edge of my fingernail that had pooled onto the wood.

"You don't need to worry," he said, his voice soft. "We don't believe in *kyranas*."

I closed my eyes.

"Surely you know that," he finished.

"I know," I said, though my voice sounded harsh, a little defensive.

"The days of blood mates are long past. The gods and goddesses of Krynn do not look after Allavar, nor its people. That's not to say…"

I turned back to him. Despite his sorry state, despite the infection that was heating his body from the inside out, I would've had to be blind to ignore the curved outline of his erection against my sheets. He brought a knee up when he noticed my straying gaze, and I bit my lip, my hands fluttering at my sides, unsure what to do with them.

"That's not to say what?" I asked, scrambling for words.

He blew out a rough breath. "That's not to say that there are not remnants of it that linger like stardust in the air. Allavar is a strange place. This land is infused with magic that beings from all over the universe have tried to study, to capture, to quantify. And that is only in the Above."

I swallowed hard. "What…what does that have to do with *kyranas*?"

"Nothing and everything," he replied, the corner of his lip quirking. His riddles again. "Maybe it's magic why you call to me. Why I would know your scent anywhere. Why your blood tastes like ambrosia. Why I'm craving it even now after I've gotten my fill."

I stared at him in surprise, his gentle words like a song that threaded musically through my ears, down my throat, and fluttered in my belly.

"I don't know if my ancestors knew what they were doing,

mating with the Allavari. What that bloodline would create. Even still, the Allavari blood tames those berserker rages and the strength a Kylorr would get from a *kyranas'* blood. Those baser, primal parts of ourselves are *tempered* with magic, not fed. Kylorr of old could have razed down an entire city on the blood of their *kyrana*. Me?" His smile returned, easy but tired. "I only wish to listen to your voice and let it lull me back to sleep, though I am sated on your blood. Does that make you feel better, little witch?"

No.

"A little," I said. Mindlessly, I scraped at more wax on the table. "There are some Kylorr in Rolara who still believe in *kyranas.*"

"And who am I dissuade them?" Lorik asked. "But a *kyrana* pairing has not been reported in Allavar in nearly three hundred years, when the portal to the Below was reopened. They can believe what they want. Me? I think it's more romantic to choose your mate, not have one be chosen for you. What do you think?"

I chuckled, some of the tension leaving my shoulders. The tingling sensation was beginning to ebb, and I felt more grounded, my heart beginning to steady.

"So when you feed on blood normally…" I trailed off. "It feels like that?"

Lorik's gaze burned. "I didn't say that."

Oh.

"It's like attraction," he said. "A Kylorr will like the taste of someone and not another. You?" He blew out a rough breath, his leg shifting underneath the sheet. "I like your blood very, very much, Marion. We fit one another in that way. It's natural. It's not *uncommon*, but no, it doesn't happen every time. I've only experienced it once before."

"A lover?" I asked before I thought better of it.

He smiled, watching me. His teeth seemed sharper in the low light, but I couldn't find it in me to be afraid.

"Yes."

I nodded.

"Have you ever been fed from before?" he wanted to know.

"Once," I told him. "My sister, Aysia."

His brow furrowed. "Was she sick?"

I knew why he was asking. It wasn't common practice to feed on a family member unless the circumstances were dire.

"She was dying. It...it didn't save her," I said quietly.

His wings twitched. "I'm sorry, Marion."

"It was a long time ago," I told him. Ten years. "And it's not a secret. She wasn't my sister by blood. Only in..." My soul, my heart. "Only in every way it actually mattered."

"What happened to her?" Lorik asked. I continued to scrape my nail across the wood, though no more wax remained. "I've heard rumors, but...you never truly know."

"She fell in love," I told him, trying to keep the bitterness out of my voice.

"With...Veras?"

I nodded, hating that name. Hating that Allavari male and his slick smile with every fiber of my being. The hate had never dulled. Not a single bit.

"Yes. And it got her killed," I told him. "I'm a healer, and I couldn't save her."

CHAPTER 8

I woke with a crick in my neck, but the heavy blanket from my bed draped over my shoulders. It took me a moment to gain my bearings—I was sitting in the chair I'd been perched in the majority of yesterday with a stiff back. Morning light streamed across an empty bed from the window behind me.

Lorik.

I stood, noticing the coverlet had been replaced and was smoothed. Not a single sound came from within my cottage, and I walked to the door, peering into the kitchen, finding it empty.

The fire in the hearth was burning, though, keeping the chill of wintry air away. Soon, all of Allavar would be covered in snow.

"Lorik?" I called out, thinking he might be in the washroom, only to receive no response. I frowned.

When I opened the door to my cottage, tugging on my soft boots and grabbing a shawl to wrap around my shoulders from where it hung off the back of the chair, I stepped onto the cobbled path and peered around.

Surely he didn't simply leave without saying goodbye, I thought, a dull disappointment throbbing in my chest, though I should've been happy to have my bed back.

Sighing, I went around the side of the cottage...

Only to find Lorik standing in the middle of my garden, peering at the glowfly hives.

He was glorious in sunlight. I couldn't help but admire him. His wings were completely stretched out as if he was warming them in the morning sun. I could see the veins in the dark gray membranes. They resembled roots of a plant, of a tree, decorating his wings.

He was bare-chested, I realized, likely because I had yet to wash his shirt and vest, still covered in blood. I felt a pang of guilt at the thought, hurried back inside to snag the coverlet from the bed, and returned.

I was certain he'd heard me before, but this time he turned to greet me. I was pleased to note that he looked significantly better this morning—more akin to the confident, mischievous male I'd admired in the market.

His eyes looked bright though they were no longer swirling with color. His skin was luminous—an Allavari trait I'd always envied—and his straight, dark hair was gleaming. The fresh bandage on his wound was clean, no signs of bleeding after I'd stitched it the morning before when he'd slept.

Maybe all he needed was another feeding, I couldn't help but think. Could I have prevented his suffering yesterday?

"Good morning," I greeted, a little shy. I held up the blanket, and Lorik frowned at it before understanding crossed his face.

"Worried about me, little witch?"

Had his cheeks darkened slightly? Despite his teasing words, he turned and folded his wings against his back. I stared at the suede-like flesh covering the thick bones of them. Though Aysia had been part Kylorr, she'd taken more of the Allavari blood of her mother. She hadn't had wings, nor had any of the children at Correl's orphanage.

With the exception of a Kylorr female I'd stitched up six years ago, this was the closest I'd ever been to wings.

"You can touch them if you'd like," came Lorik's voice. His tone gruff and husky, dipped down like a lover's in bed. I hadn't been with a male in years—hadn't touched or stroked or kissed or laughed with one in bed in years—and I'd never felt the stretch of time more than right then.

Without agonizing over whether this was appropriate or not, I reached out my fingertips before I could second guess myself. He'd given me permission…and I was endlessly curious.

Lorik shivered when the heat of my fingers stroked down the membrane of one wing. The skin was surprisingly soft until it met the hard bone of the skeletal structure. I could feel the tiny veins running beneath it, just as I could see them in the sun.

"Are you sensitive here?" I asked. Lorik huffed out a deep breath. I realized belatedly that my voice was as low as his had been. This moment felt entirely too intimate, and I swallowed as I let my hand lower.

"Yes," he replied. That was all he would say, and I hurriedly draped the coverlet over his shoulders, standing on my tiptoes to reach them. Wrapped around his wings, the coverlet made a ridiculous shape, but when he faced me again, I wrapped the front together, tucking it tight.

I could feel him watching me as I fussed over him. Did he *like* it when I fussed over him?

"I'll have your clothes washed today," I told him, grasping for something to say, chancing a peek up at him. His blue eyes were swirling again.

"If you wanted me naked, Marion, you only had to ask," he said. "We can burn my clothes instead if you wish. I won't complain."

"Be serious," I chided though I felt my lips quirking at the edges. When the coverlet was secure and I was satisfied he wouldn't freeze in the chilly morning air, I stepped back. Only he snatched my wrist, quicker than I could blink—frighteningly fast—and kept me against him. Pulled me even closer. "Lorik."

"You've given me your blanket—what's going to keep you warm besides me?" he wondered, tucking me into his side like I belonged there. His skin was so hot against me I was worried he was feverish again. "I'm fine. I run hotter than most," he told me, as if reading my mind.

"What…what are you doing out here this early?" I asked, letting him warm me. He'd tucked the coverlet around me so I didn't have anywhere to turn…but it felt wonderful. The heat of him contrasted with the icy air across my cheeks. I wondered if he'd bathed already because he smelled clean and fresh, no lingerings of poison or infection.

He would leave soon, I knew. There would be no reason for him to stay.

"Tell me about the glowflies," he murmured, nudging his chin toward the five nearly hidden hives on the outskirts of the garden. Each hive was situated close to their favored plant. "A peculiar hobby. An incredibly dangerous one."

"You saw them," I pointed out. "You were out here a couple nights ago with me."

"Yes," he said, "but I knew better than to get too close."

"Afraid of glowflies?" I asked, my tone teasing. I felt relaxed against him. This newness, this unpredictability when it came to him was exciting. Exhilarating. I wondered if he'd steal a kiss while he had me close.

I was so used to being alone…and I was used to Allavari men. Most were too proper that it bordered on being cold. Most didn't show their feelings and very rarely acted on them. Allavari, like the Kylorr, were raised to show little emotion. To never let anyone see you struggle because that was not the Allavari way.

"Terrified," Lorik responded, and I heard the smile in his voice without looking up at him.

Most Allavari men would certainly never admit to being scared of anything after plastering a woman against them. That was what I'd always liked about Lorik. He was unpredictable.

Even in the market, when others looked at him with half-hidden wariness. Confident in himself, he didn't seem to care what others thought of him or how a certain action would be perceived.

"You have a *braydus* as a companion and glowflies as your garden keepers," Lorik said, his tone wistful. He shook his head, his good arm sliding down my spine, before he hooked a hand around my waist.

My cheeks warmed, and I grinned, trying to hide it beneath the curtain of my hair when I ducked my head.

"Are you sure you aren't from the Below after all?" he wondered.

"What do you mean?" I asked.

"Glowflies, like your *braydus*, were once native to the Below," he told me. "How do you think they have all their magic? They are literally bound in it."

I looked up at him. "You sure know a lot about the Below and all its creatures."

"Oh, I'm an expert."

"I've never heard that before," I told him. "Glowflies are rare, yes. But I managed to collect all of them from across the Black Veil, re-homing them here. I chose this place to build my cottage because there was already a wrathweed hive lodged in the trunk of that tree there and a patch of the stuff growing wild."

I gestured to the tall river tree on the west of the property. I'd dug out the hive and moved it years ago, but the hollow in the trunk remained.

"Peek likes to lie in there sometimes. His little hideaway," I told Lorik.

Lorik waved his bad arm—making him wince—toward the cottage, toward the bench he'd been sitting on a couple nights ago.

"Your *braydus* has been watching my every move," he informed me.

Sure enough, Peek was sitting on the bench, staring right at

Lorik, his long tail curled around his legs. His ears were straight up in the air. Though Peek had slept in the bedroom last night, he'd always been on alert—a stranger in his domain, no doubt, making him uneasy.

"He's keeping the Severs away, remember?" I teased.

Lorik's jaw tightened. He looked back to the hives, evenly spaced around the night garden. "Wrathweed. Fire cup. Brightbell?"

He looked to me in confirmation as he gestured. I nodded.

"Death needle. Which makes that one the shadevine hive," Lorik continued, looking at the pitch black teardrop-shaped mass on the edge of the garden. At night, it glowed silver from within.

"Yes, that's right."

"Wherever did you find that one?" he asked.

Shadevines were the rarest of the glowflies.

"It was easy," I told him. "Utterly by chance, I suppose. I was out in the forest collecting lovery leaves for my candles. Before I knew it, night had fallen. But there was a cave nearby, and it was glowing silver in the dark. I saw the shadevines creeping along the rock. I knew there must be a hive inside. I went back the next day when they were asleep and started the transfer."

"Is the cave still there?" he wondered.

"Yes, but there was only one hive in the cave. I haven't come across another in the five years I've had this one."

"Shadevine queens are immortal," he said softly. "You'd think there would be more since that's the case."

There was something in the tone of his voice that had me quieting.

"Yes, but many queens were captured to try to replicate that immortality," I said carefully.

The Rolara villagers knew I kept glowflies or at least suspected I did. The antidotes and some of my potions couldn't be possible without them. There were others who kept glowflies. The Healers' Guild, for instance, kept a patch of land on the northern edge of the Black Veil and tended to it in shifts based off the season. I was the only one who had shadevines, as far as I knew. But I had never been selfish. Any request from the guild for shadevine blooms, I'd honored.

"Why are you asking about the shadevine hive?"

I'd had three trespassers on my land in the ten years I'd lived in the Black Veil. All of them had come for the glowflies. Foolishly, they'd all come at night, when the glowflies were active, and they'd been stung dozens of times each, every hive swarming as if they knew they needed to protect themselves as a single unit. The village witch's barrier spell only worked on Severs, apparently. Not thieves.

One thief had *died*. I'd heard about it in the village next day. Wrathweed stings were poisonous. To be stung thrice without an antidote was certain death. Since then, not a single soul had tried to take the hives.

I didn't know if the thieves had wanted the shadevines or if they'd wanted the hearts of the hives—where most of the magic was concentrated and were thus most valuable. Likely, they'd wanted both.

"Curiosity," Lorik answered me.

"Many have tried to take them," I informed him, keeping my tone level. "None have succeeded."

"That's apparent," he replied. "They trust their keepers alone. You must have a pure soul, Marion."

I cocked my head to the side. He was still radiating heat. I felt the rumble of his voice against me, the vibration of it sinking into my skin.

He was…*something*. Something I couldn't see. I knew that as certainly as I knew I *should* stay away from him.

So why was I pressing closer, pleased with his compliment? Maybe I'd been much too starved for affection and intimacy. Maybe I missed the heat and weight of a male against me. Maybe just one little taste of Lorik would be enough.

But I was a healer first and foremost. I couldn't forget that. I needed to see him well…and then afterward?

Maybe afterward I could explore whatever this was. Maybe afterward, I could go to Grimstone's with him and drink ale and kiss him in a back booth.

I wanted to uncover all his secrets…even if I feared what I would find.

CHAPTER 9

Lorik was watching me, lounging against one of the largest river trees on my property. His broad back was to the trunk, and he had one knee brought up, his bad arm resting against it. Similar in position to how I'd found him in the Black Veil three nights ago.

"Stop," I said, though I was trying to hide my smile as I dumped the bedding into the basin.

"Stop what?" he asked innocently. He'd chosen that tree to relax against because it was closest to the washing tub I had outside—a wide, hollowed-out tree trunk that I believed had been struck by lightning once. It was a perfect depth to let the bedding soak in.

After Lorik's infection had passed, the sheets and the coverlet needed a desperate wash. But the afternoon was fading, the sun already beginning to lower in the sky, so I wanted to take advantage before the night chill set in.

"Stop looking at me," I replied. "Stop smiling."

He grinned in response.

"I like looking at you," he told me. "Why does it bother you?"

"Because...because..." I trailed off, uncertain how to respond. It sounded ridiculous, even to my own ears. But how could I tell him that every time he looked at me, I felt *consumed*? How could I tell him that he made me nervous, shy, and elated all at once?

"Because you're not used to it," he murmured. "You live out here, alone. My beautiful little witch in the woods. You need to be appreciated. You need to be touched. I think you need to be loved."

I stopped mixing the soapy water in the trunk to look at him in surprise.

He smirked. "You need a lover, Marion."

"Are you volunteering for the job?" I asked, flustered but quirking a brow with more confidence than I felt.

I'd meant it as a tease, but Lorik said, "Yes."

The word was soft in its seriousness.

"Humans can be so strange about sex," he added. "Even if they grew up on Allavar."

"And I would argue that Allavari are even more strange about it. Private," I told him, looking back down at the basin. "Don't you think? You're part Allavari, aren't you?"

"Once," he replied, his tone breezy.

"You always say things like that," I pointed out. "Things that never make sense and are only meant to confuse."

"Maybe I want to keep you guessing," he said. "Keep the mystery alive."

"Oh, it's well and alive, Lorik Ravael."

"Maybe I'm boring. Maybe I'm quite dull to be around when I'm not suffering from a botched poisoning."

A poisoning you won't tell me much about, I thought silently.

"I want to know what you look like unleashed."

Unable to keep the small gasp from escaping, I darted my gaze up at him again.

"Maybe that's the once Kylorr in me though," he added. "So

yes, I think you don't like when I look at you like this…because I'm looking at you in a very particular way, Marion. I always have, haven't I?"

A memory from the market rose. Of Lorik leaning against the wall of the local apothecary shop, arms crossed over his chest. I'd caught him looking at me, but instead of being embarrassed, he'd tilted his chin up, that familiar sinful, flirtatious smile spreading across his lips. I'd been too shocked, too flustered, too excited that I'd looked away quickly.

Had that been an invitation?

Of course it'd been, you daft fool, I thought. But what had I done? I'd avoided his gaze, sold the last of my potions, packed up my supplies, and fled back to the Black Veil. Because it was familiar. It was safe.

Ever since Aysia, I'd never wanted to be in love. Love made a fool out of anyone it touched. It addled your brain; it was addicting like a drug.

More often than not, it left you brokenhearted. Or…dead.

"Tell me a secret, little witch," he murmured in the sudden quiet. I couldn't hear the birds or the wind or the scampering of Peek as he tried to catch a ground critter.

"You frighten me," I told him.

He grinned again, but this time his teeth seemed sharper and his eyes gleamed in the lowering sunlight. With his sharp, proud features, he looked every bit the arrogant Allavari noble. Allavari were snobbish about bloodlines. I wondered about his…because he wasn't a commoner—that was for certain.

"It's probably best that I do," he answered.

A lengthy silence passed after those words. I didn't understand him. One moment he was telling me he wanted to see me *unleashed*…the next it felt like he was trying to warn me away.

The soapy water was icy in the basin, and I squeezed my fists together to get the blood flowing before I needed to start scrubbing the sheets.

"Here," he murmured. "Allow me."

I frowned, watching as he maneuvered himself toward me, all languid grace for someone so tall and large. When he reached the basin, he spread his palm across the surface of the water.

"What are you...?" I trailed off, my lips parting when I saw steam rise from the surface and an unseen current underwater jostle the fabric. "Lorik! Save your energy. This doesn't matter."

"It's a small thing," he replied, taking back his hand though the sheets continued to move in the basin. "Now your hands won't be cold."

And I realized it *was* a small thing for him. I'd...I'd never seen...

It had hardly *phased* him.

"You wouldn't let me wash the sheets. You nearly took my head off when I asked," he rasped, meeting my eyes. "At least allow me to warm the water for you and lessen the work."

"I've never seen anyone channel their magic so quickly," I commented, my hands hovering above the water as I knelt beside the hollow trunk. "That kind of magic is..."

Lorik leveled me a careful look. "The Allavari have lost their way. They've forgotten."

"Forgotten what?" I asked, dumbfounded.

"Forgotten that magic is as natural as the air we breathe," he told me. "This land is special, every layer of it. It's alive. Even you have magic, Marion. It's grown in you since you were born on Allavar. You pull it up from the ground you stand on, you fill your lungs with it in the sunlight, and you feel it drift over your skin like a silk sheet when you sleep."

My lips parted. "I'm human. I don't have magic. Not like the Allavari. I certainly can't do"—I gestured to the basin—"*that*."

"But you can keep all five species of glowflies successfully and befriend a *braydus*. Those are magical creatures, and they recognize that magic in *you*. Have you ever thought it strange that they allow you so close?"

"There are people in the Healers' Guild who keep glowflies," I pointed out. "And I'm certainly not the first to have a *braydus* as a companion."

Right?

Lorik went quiet as he studied me. Finally, he said, "Think what you wish, Marion. You say I can channel magic better than anyone you've seen? That's because I understand that magic is an extension of myself, that it is rooted as deeply in me as I am in it. I understand there is balance in it. I don't fight that. That's something the Above world has also forgotten."

The Above world?

"Taking without reciprocation only depletes magic. It needs to be refueled. Did you know that your cottage, your land has more magic than I've felt in the Black Veil? Than I've ever felt in Rolara?"

"Is that really true?"

He inclined his head. "Because you've allowed magic to bloom here—the glowflies being a large part of that. You tend to them, they produce for you. A symbiotic relationship. And you don't expect more than they can give. A beautiful balance. You've done well here, Marion."

That compliment was perhaps more flattering than any I'd heard from him. Even beyond the warmth I'd felt when he'd called me beautiful.

"Thank you," I said softly. "That means a lot."

His lips curled in a gentle smile. "There's nothing to thank me for. It's merely the truth."

The sheets were still swirling in the basin, the water so hot it was practically simmering. I wondered how much effort that had taken him, when he should've been channeling every last scrap of energy into resting and healing. He was much better than he'd been yesterday, obviously. But I didn't want him to take another sudden turn.

I was just about to ask him when he wanted to feed next, the question perched on the edge of my tongue, when his head snapped toward the Black Veil, his pointed ears twitching, the muscles in his chest bunching.

"What is it?" I asked, slight trepidation in my tone. "A Sever?"

"Too early for the veil to lift," he murmured, his tone distracted. "But someone is nearing. I can feel them."

Lorik stood in a graceful rise, silent despite his bulk. His wings unfurled, stretching in the late sun. I stayed kneeling at the basin, eyeing the property line, where the protection spell had been placed. But now…doubt had begun to creep in my mind. Was Lorik right? Was the spell even real? Or was it *Peek*? The protection spell certainly hadn't helped against the thieves…only the Severs.

We heard a pair of men approach my cottage, and with dread and bitterness building in my gut, I realized who it was.

Veras.

The Allavari crime lord parading himself around as a noble.

Veras, who my sister had fallen in love with. The head-over-heels, insane kind of love, where nothing else had mattered to her except him.

Veras, who'd ultimately gotten Aysia killed.

CHAPTER 10

"How dare you show your face here," I said quietly, not moving from my position at the basin, staring at Veras from across the clearing. "*Again.* I warned you once before."

Veras was a handsome full-blooded Allavari male. His skin gleamed, not a blemish or scar marring his face. His silky, pin-straight hair tumbled down his back in a silver waterfall, the tips of his sharp ears poking out on both sides of his head. His lavender-colored irises might've been mesmerizing if I didn't want to tear them from his skull.

He was dressed in impeccable Allavari silk, stitched with delicate metal beads which made a vine pattern. His pants were creased cleanly, his boots shining, though I delighted that a scuff of mud covered the toe. Veras would hate that if he noticed—appearance was everything for someone like him.

When I saw the beautiful wreath of goldwood blooms and lakelight leaves, bound and entwined in a silver ring decorated with blue jewels, my mood only darkened. My sister's favorites. I knew why he was here.

"If you had let me bury her at my estate, Marion, I

wouldn't need to trek all the way out to the Black Veil," he returned, his voice calm, matter-of-fact. But Veras wasn't even looking at me. He was looking at Lorik, who'd stepped in front of me.

Veras had one of his guards with him. A burly Ernitian-Kylorr male from the looks of him, all muscle and mass, with a pair of giant wings tucked against his back.

"Lorik Ravael," Veras purred. "You were the last person I expected to see here. Actually, I take that back. We are in the Black Veil, after all."

I cut a look to Lorik, but his eyes were only narrowed on the intruder. His arms came across his chest. His bare chest, I realized, and I saw Veras note that too.

Veras said looked back to me and said, "Ignore me, Marion. I'm just passing through."

"You can't just come here whenever you wish," I told him, finally standing so he wouldn't see me kneeling any longer. I rounded Lorik, my pace quick toward Veras. "Enough of this charade already. It's been *ten years.*"

Veras smiled at me. "I don't do this to torment you, Marion, despite what you think. I commissioned the wreath. The lakelight leaves are beautiful this time of year, and I know Aysia always thought so."

"*Don't* you dare," I said quietly.

Veras went still. I saw his jaw tick. Up close, I noticed lines beginning to form around his mouth and eyes—lines I'd never noticed before.

"Ten years is a long time, yes," he said. "But it would take more than a lifetime for me to forget your sister."

"What would your newest lover think about that?" I wondered. His guard stepped closer to me, but then Lorik was there, pushing him back. The guard had nearly fifty pounds of bulk on Lorik, but there was something about his expression that told me Lorik would win any fight he started. Something unseen, especially given how quickly he could channel magic—a skill I hadn't seen even in the highest of Allavari.

Veras held up his free hand, and his guard stepped away.

"We're just passing through," Veras said again, but this time, his lavender eyes were pinned on Lorik. "We don't want trouble."

"Neither did she," I couldn't help but bite back.

Veras's gaze shuttered. His chin tilted back, and I saw the way his throat bobbed when he swallowed.

"I only want to make the offering, Marion," he finally said, his voice steeling. His tone was clipped. Final. "Nothing more."

Out of the corner of my eye, I saw Lorik regard me. Waiting for what I would say? I couldn't help but remember his offer to me. That all I had to do was ask and he'd give me whatever I asked of him in repayment for helping him.

In the beginning of their relationship, I'd never liked Veras. But I thought that had had more to do with Aysia and me than him. He was a dangerous Allavari male with more than questionable morals. But Aysia had loved him, and that was the only reason I allowed him to make his offerings on my land…where she was buried.

"A Sever will take it anyway," I said, looking down at the wreath.

"One might. But they know better to stay down Below where they belong. Despite what you think, I've always looked after you, Marion. Aysia would want that," Veras said. "Some advice? Stay away from this one."

He swept a hand toward Lorik. A warning growl rose up from the Kylorr-Allavari male, a sound I'd never heard from him before.

Veras continued, "You think *I'm* bad? You should look at the company you keep."

I stiffened. "*Leave.* And never come back."

"Not before I give my offering," he growled. "How long will it take for you to understand that we are bound, Marion? Bound by Aysia? I will *never* abandon her, just as you never will. How many times have I expressed my regret and grief over what happened? When will it be enough for you? You think I'm the villain in this, and that's true…but *you* will never be able to forgive. And it will eat at you for the rest of your days. Despite what you think, *I don't want that.*"

I felt the blood drain from my face. Fury and disbelief and grief and sadness and bitterness swarmed within me until I was rooted into place. Frozen. Unable to move.

Lorik moved for me. He stepped forward, eye to eye with Veras, blocking me from view with the expanse of his wings.

"She asked you to leave. So leave…before blood is spilled at her feet in payment. I am not bound by the laws of the Allavari, remember?"

There was a dangerous edge in Lorik's voice that nearly had *me* shuddering. Dark and deep, the words left no room for response. Even the guard Veras had brought with him flinched back.

Veras didn't speak. He stepped around Lorik and placed the wreath at my feet, his jaw tight, his movements stiff.

"Make the offering yourself, Marion," Veras murmured. "They were her favorite. You know that."

I had half a mind to rip up the wreath into a million tiny pieces…but his words kept ringing through my mind: *But you will never be able to forgive. And it will eat at you for the rest of your days.*

Was he right? Would I hold this hatred and bitterness with me until the day I left this life? Would I carry the resentment and grief into the *next* life?

I didn't want that, I realized as I stared at the wreath at my feet. I didn't want that at all.

"She died a terrible death because of you. I don't know if I can forgive you, Veras. Ever," I said quietly. Lorik turned. I felt the heat of his hand come around my waist. Veras paused on the pathway, looking back at me over his shoulder. "I loved her more than anything in this world."

"What you don't understand, Marion," he replied, "is that I did too. We have that in common, at the very least."

I choked out a huffed sigh, feeling tears burn the backs of my eyes…and I didn't want him to see me cry. Not then, not ever.

Thankfully, he turned, his guard trailing him, and he was gone a moment later. Only then could I breathe again.

CHAPTER 11

"Marion."

I started at the voice, turning to regard Lorik, who stood on the edge of the clearing. My sister's grave was a few stones' throw away from my cottage, beyond the protection spell's barrier but shielded by a circle of giant river trees with thick, velvety leaves. Through the thick boughs, I could spy the golden light pouring from my cottage windows and realized it was night already.

How long had I been standing here?

Veras had purchased the white, thick columns and the decorative headstone, etched in the finest of silver Allavari metals. I had refused initially, but like always, he never cared what I wanted. He'd done it anyway. Her shrine. There was even a little pedestal for an offering. I usually placed bright, fragrant sprigs of whatever forest flowers I found during my foraging or a few biscuits, mixed with currants and nuts, that I'd baked that day.

It was a beautiful grave, even I had to admit it. More than I'd ever be able to afford for her. Aysia had liked that about Veras. That he'd spoiled her because she'd grown up with nothing except stolen bracelets and lashings when she'd stayed outside too late.

He had given her the world, laid it at her feet like he'd laid the wreath at mine.

"Such sad eyes, little witch," Lorik commented, his tone gentle.

He stepped toward me, his blue orbs even more vibrant in the darkness. It always seemed to me that he grew stronger in the dark. His footsteps were sure, his back straight, his wings flared. He looked *normal*. Healthy, even, despite the bandage on his shoulder, one I'd forgotten to check and poultice this afternoon.

"What can I do to make you feel better?"

"I'm sorry," I said, shaking my head. "I lost track of time."

"Don't apologize to me when you have nothing to be sorry for," he said firmly. His eyes strayed down to what I was holding in my hands. "Do you want me to destroy that? Bury it far away? Set it on fire, perhaps? Fly it up to the Massadian Mountains and drop it off the cliff?"

Confused, I looked down and saw I was still holding on to Veras's wreath. I choked out a small, disbelieving laugh, surprised by the suggestions though they helped cut through the daze I'd found myself in.

"No, no," I finally said, giving him a small, shy smile. "That won't be necessary. I'll make the offering, just as Veras wanted."

"Is that what you want?" he asked.

"He's right," I said quietly. My mind had been racing ever since he'd left. It had never stopped. I felt drained. I felt… strangely at peace. "She would have loved this wreath. She loved nature. She loved being in nature, being outside. She would collect lakelight leaves when they turned color this time of year and make a crown of them. She did that every single year and then hung them to dry so she'd be able to look at their color until the next season. I still have them somewhere—all these dried crowns she wove, likely crumbled to dust in a chest."

"It's all right to be angry at him, Marion," Lorik told me. "I don't know the specifics, but I heard about what happened in

Rolara—villagers talk. He was careless. He didn't protect her when he should have."

"I've been angry for so long," I whispered. "I'm tired of it."

Lorik's hand came to the middle of my back, and I pressed myself into him without a moment's hesitation. He slid it down until it curled around my hip.

"Do you find it difficult to forgive those who have hurt you?" he asked. His tone was careful, evenly measured. The question struck me as earnest, almost solemn.

"Yes," I confessed. Lorik blew out a sharp breath. "I try so hard not to hurt other people. I'm careful with my words, I consider their feelings in everything I do, even at the cost to me sometimes. So when other people hurt me, nothing feels worse."

"Being hurt is a natural part of life, Marion," he informed me. "The Kylorr have a saying—*from blood, you overcome*. You need to be cut deeply in order to be strong."

"And that's where I'm weakest, I think," I told him. "I'm a healer because I didn't like to see Aysia cry at night when Correl would punish her. I'm a healer because my nature is not to harm but to heal. So why I can't heal myself?"

"Oh, my love," Lorik said, his tone gruff. And I realized I liked that term of endearment entirely too much coming off his lips. "There's a part of me that just wants to keep you shielded from every dark thing in this world. Even me."

Looking up at him in surprise, I saw something flicker over his face. A shimmering.

"But that would be a lie. That would be a disservice to you," he continued. "If you were mine, I'd want to protect you without keeping you caged to keep you safe. Perhaps Veras was trying to do the same with Aysia. Only he didn't protect her enough. Would you have rather he kept her tucked away in his estate? So not even a splinter could have pricked her?"

"No, of course not," I said quietly, sighing. "But it was much more than a splinter that killed her."

"Do you think you'll ever forgive him?" Lorik wondered, his eyes shifting to Aysia's grave. Moonlight speared the headstone, and the metal shimmered and gleamed. How could I have let so much time get away from me?

"I don't know," I said. "But I do know that I can't do this anymore. Every time I see him, every time I hear his name in the village, I get so angry. And it affects me. Like today—I've been standing here for hours, and I didn't even realize it. This hatred is taking away my life, and I don't want to let it anymore.

"So I don't know if I can forgive him, but I've decided I'm going to try to move on from the past. Because he's right…I know he did love her. Deeply. He made her very happy, even though the end was tumultuous between us. I can't just erase that. She *chose* him. I can accept that. And we have our love for her in common, and so he will always be part of my life, no matter how much I wish he wasn't."

"I think that's a good start," Lorik murmured.

"It's the only thing I can think to do anymore," I said. Sighing, I dusted off dirt and shriveled, wrinkled leaves from the pedestal and lay the wreath on top. It must have cost Veras more than I made at the market in three months.

Lorik's warm hand never left my waist. I shivered when a breeze wound through my hair and turned into him. My emotions were a little raw tonight, but it was nice to have someone near. To be able to lean on someone else, allow them to be my pillar, when I'd never had anyone like that before.

"You have a pure soul, Marion," Lorik told me gently as he led me from the clearing. "I told you earlier—kind and gentle. There are not many like you in the world, especially here on Allavar. You're as rare as the creatures you so lovingly keep."

"But?" I asked, hearing that unspoken word in his voice.

His smile was a half one, not quite reaching his eyes as they scanned the darkness of the Black Veil.

"I'm worried that someone like me isn't good for someone

like you," he confessed. "I worry for the day when you look at me like you look at Veras."

I stilled. I hadn't expected the *vulnerability* I heard in his gruff tone.

I wasn't a fool. I knew there was a lot lurking beneath the surface of Lorik Ravael. Unspoken, dangerous truths. Even Veras's guard had been afraid of him. The barbed words edged in warning from Veras told me that even he knew something I didn't.

There was a suspicion nagging in my mind, but it was too ridiculous to even voice. That Lorik had dealings with the Severs, which was forbidden. Anyone who came across Severs were never seen or heard from again.

Like Merec? I wondered, remembering what Lorik had told me about the old shopkeeper.

"What did Veras mean?" I asked quietly. Lorik's hand tightened on my waist. "When he said he wasn't surprised to see you in the Black Veil?"

"I hunt in the forest sometimes," Lorik replied.

"You two know one another?"

"Not in the way you suspect, little witch," he replied, cutting me a sharp glance out of the corner of his eye. "We've encountered one another in the village at times, nothing more. I didn't lie to you about my dealings with him. I truly have none."

"He seems to hold a strong opinion about you," I commented.

"Most do."

"And why is that?"

Lorik stilled on the path before turning to face me. We lingered inside the line of trees that wound around my cottage, just outside the protection barrier spell.

"Because most Allavari don't trust what they don't understand," Lorik told me. "And most of them do not understand me. They don't understand why I don't kiss the ass of every noble I encounter, why I don't involve myself with their celebrations and affairs, why I don't live in Rolara, why they never see me with a lover, a friend, or family. To them, I am *other*. I always have been and I always will be. It's not my duty to make them understand me. I simply couldn't care less."

My gaze dropped to his lips as he spoke. He must've washed while I'd been visiting Aysia's grave. The ends of his hair were damp, and he smelled of my soap, infused with whitedrop oil.

"But you…" Lorik said. "I care about what you think of me, Marion."

"You do?"

He nodded. "You're the only one I can say that about in Rolara."

"We know so little about one another. How can you say that?"

"Sometimes you just know, little witch. Attraction is fairly easy to ascertain," Lorik said, his hand sliding up my back, making me shiver. When his hand trailed up my neck and his shorn claws scraped pleasurably against my scalp, I nearly gasped. My throat seemed to tingle with that sweet touch. "And I'm certainly attracted to you. But connection? A true connection? That's rare. But I have it with you. Do you feel it too?"

My heart was thumping in my chest.

"Yes," I whispered.

The sound he made was a cross between a purr and a growl. "Mmm, I'm glad."

The smile that crossed my face was perhaps the first genuine smile since Veras had arrived, and it felt goofy and too wide, stretching my features until I thought they might crack.

"You're a beautiful woman," Lorik told me, watching me quietly. I got the strangest sense that he was soaking in my smile, enjoying it, savoring it. There was patience lining the sharp bones of his face, as if we had all the time in the world, lingering on the edge of my cottage's land. "I hope you know that."

"Thank you," I said quietly. "You are too."

Lorik's brow raised, and my face flamed.

"Not a woman, obviously. Beautiful, yes," I said hurriedly. I laughed through my mortification. "Gods, I'm terrible at this."

"You think I'm beautiful?" Lorik teased.

"You know you are," I said, still recovering from my blunder. "You know the effect you have on people. I've seen it."

Lorik took pity on me. He leaned down, and I held my breath, wondering if he would try to steal a kiss, as he'd already threatened.

I was both disappointed and immensely caught off guard when he brushed his lips across my temple. His lips were soft and warm. He let them linger there before kissing my forehead, holding me in place with the hand still tangled in my hair.

Then I felt him tense, his muscles going tight against me.

"What's wrong?" I asked, pulling back with my flushed cheeks on display, frowning.

Lorik was looking at something in the forest. When I turned, the breath in my lungs turned to ice.

Glowing blue eyes were watching us from the darkness. A hulking creature with a hunched back stepped forward, its tattered cloak billowing out from behind it.

A Sever.

CHAPTER 12

I'd only ever seen Severs from a distance. Through thick trees, walking aimlessly in the forest, and only ever at night.

But this one was so close I could practically smell it—like rotting leaves and forest decay. Sweet, almost. Sickeningly pungent.

It was lurching toward us, its heavy feet crunching over branches that splintered like bone.

The Sever's skin was a pale gray, nearly translucent. Black veins spread underneath the flesh, like the veins of Lorik's wings. Dark horns were curled back from his head, one broken in half. The Sever didn't have any wings, but there seemed to be something protruding beneath its cloak where they may have once been. Cut?

It looked like Lorik. An Allavari-Kylorr male, only…a horrific version of one, as if it had been living in darkness, consumed by something unseen. It looked like its flesh was rotting away, its bones too sharp. I almost felt pity for the Sever, until it began to make a dull hiss in the back of its throat, its pace quickening toward us, scarred arm outstretched.

Peek pounced into the clearing, his fur standing up, a low

growl rumbling from his chest. My *braydus*'s eyes were pinned on the Sever, and he slowly stalked toward it.

"Peek, no!"

"Get inside the cottage, Marion," Lorik told me, maneuvering me around him so he was between the Sever and me. "*Now.*"

"But Peek—"

"I'll take care of him. Go!"

I only hesitated for another moment before I darted away. There was some part of me that trusted Lorik. I wouldn't leave my *braydus* with him if I didn't, I realized.

When I made it to my cottage, I bolted the door and scurried to the chest I kept tucked underneath the counter. There was a bow and a quiver of wooden arrows inside. I was a fairly decent shot, my hands steady, though they were trembling now. I could still smell the Sever in my nostrils, churning my belly.

I went to the window, pushing the glass forward on its rusty hinges. I could hear horrible sounds in the darkness: the Sever's hiss that made the hairs on my arm stand on end, Peek's warbling growls, and the quick gust of wings. Lorik.

He was weaponless. I went back to the door, throwing it open.

"Lorik, I have—"

I stilled on the path. I hadn't made it even a few feet when I heard the sickening crunch. It happened so quickly. But I watched as Lorik made a quick twist of his hands around the Sever's neck, popped off its head like it was a doll's stuffed with feathers. The Sever's body slumped to the earth, and it lay still on the edge of the forest. The wet plop of its decapitated head joined it.

Lorik's sharp breath seemed to reach me, even from a distance away. His eyes were glowing in the darkness, like one of the glowflies' hives at midnight.

In the quiet, I watched as Peek investigated the remains,

sniffing the cloak before he was satisfied, sitting at Lorik's feet. The quiver and the bow felt entirely too useless in my hands.

"Go back inside, Marion," came Lorik's voice. Soft and incredibly gentle for someone who had just decapitated a monstrous creature with his bare hands.

And it had been easy for him, I thought.

I approached, ignoring his words.

"You're still recovering, Lorik," I said slowly, eyeing the Sever on the ground, avoiding looking at its head that had rolled near Peek. I felt oddly…calm. Was I in shock?

Lorik crouched down by the Sever, shifting its cloak so that he took hold of its arm. He pulled back the fabric, exposing the wrist.

Scars.

No…*brands*.

There were symbols etched into its skin, and Lorik huffed out a breath looking at them before he tossed the arm back to the ground with more force than necessary.

"What…what are those?"

"Crimes," Lorik answered, standing. "Marion, go back inside. I need to get rid of the body before it draws others to the area."

"Others?" I rasped. "Other Severs?"

Lorik scoffed. "This isn't a Sever. Not anymore. Or maybe he is the truest Sever, at least according to the Allavari. Get back inside and take your *braydus* with you. I'll be back soon."

Without waiting for me to respond, Lorik gathered up the Sever's limp body and its head…and shot up into the sky, the powerful gust of his wings awe-inspiring.

He disappeared overhead, the only memory of the Sever was a line of dark blood on the forest floor, which I kicked some dirt and leaves over to erase it from view. The truest Sever? Or not a Sever at all? What had he meant by that?

Peek nudged up against my leg, his big, luminous eyes staring up at me. I looked to the sky again but didn't see any sign of

Lorik. I looked around the clearing of my cottage, to the darkness of the Black Veil, which I'd never been truly frightened of before.

Now? There was an ominous feeling I couldn't help but shake. That Sever might draw others?

Hurrying back into the cottage, I made certain Peek was inside before I bolted the door. There was restless energy building in my gut. I'd been in a silent daze for most of the day, emotionally drained, and now this had happened. I paced the floor of my cottage, Peek watching me from the window sill where the glass was still open, as if he were standing guard.

It didn't take long until I heard the familiar gust of wings, until I heard a heavy weight land on the cobblestones outside my door.

"Marion," came his voice. Relief made me dizzy, and I rushed to the door, unlocking it, before Lorik stepped inside.

He smelled like the Sever, his chest smeared with its dark blood from when he'd carried it away. I didn't know what he'd done with the body. I didn't *want* to know, truthfully. Whatever he'd done, he'd done it quickly.

"Are you okay?" I rushed out, seeing a bloom of blood beneath the bandage at his shoulder. He'd torn the sutures.

"Fine," he said, tone gruff. "Are you?"

He was studying me carefully. Was he worried that I'd be frightened of him now? After what I'd seen him do?

My mind latched on to his wound. I looked at his blood-slicked chest.

"You should bathe," I told him, seeing a streak of the Sever's blood a little too close to the bandage's edge. I didn't want another infection taking root. "I'll...I'll draw a bath. And then I'll look at your shoulder."

"Marion."

"Let's get you clean, all right? You're bleeding. Then we can talk."

When I stepped into the washroom, I realized my hand was

shaking when I turned the taps. The water would be cold this time of night.

"Did you want me to heat the stones in the hearth or—"

I sucked in a sharp breath when I turned, when I heard the gentle whoosh of his pants hit the floor.

"I'll do it," he told me, standing before me fully naked, and I held my breath, hoping my face wouldn't burn right up. He maneuvered around me, all endless, muscled flesh. I was used to his bare chest, but I wasn't prepared for his bare backside, rounded but dimpled with sharp muscles at the sides. His thighs…strong and smooth.

His cock…

I swallowed, glad his attention was on the bathing tub. He skimmed his hand over the surface. Just like the washing basin outside, he heated the water quickly, steam rising with his swift magic. His soft cock swung forward with the movement, the head of it darker than the shaft.

Even soft, veins curled up the sides.

Even soft…he was shockingly large.

My nails bit into the palms of my hands. I cleared my throat, turning quickly to get a fresh bandage from my cabinet in the front room, rummaging around, clinking bottles noisily, buying time as I got my heart under control.

Just a body, I thought. As a healer, especially when I'd lived in Rolara, before I'd hidden myself away in the Black Veil, I'd seen plenty of naked bodies. Males, females—it didn't matter. They were just bodies to me. Bodies that needed tending, that needed healing, that needed care.

Lorik needs care, I told myself.

He had a beautiful body, but I reminded myself of my healer's oath and blew out a quiet breath, gathering my supplies just when I heard him sink down into the tub.

Good.

"Let me get the bandage off," I told him, eyeing him as he

leaned back in the bathing tub, his wings tucked uncomfortably inside. It was laughable small for someone his size, but at least it covered his distracting cock.

Kneeling at the side of the tub, I set my supplies next to me and unwrapped the bloodied cloth. Water trickled when he cupped some in his palms, splashing his chest to loosen and soften the Sever blood. I handed him a clean washcloth, and he began to scrub, his brow furrowed in concentration, his lips pursed in an almost pouting expression that I thought was oddly adorable.

He didn't like to be dirty, I realized.

"You tore through a few of the sutures. I'll need to redo them," I told him quietly.

He didn't say anything. In fact, he was entirely too quiet.

Lorik scrubbed at his body until not a speck of blood remained. He uncapped the bathing tub and watched the dirtied water swirl down before he turned on the taps again. He didn't even hiss when the icy water met his flesh. He didn't even shiver, keeping still as fresh water from my well rose around him.

As for me, I kept my eyes firmly on his shoulder, cutting out the threads of the sutures before threading my curved needle.

"I'll start stitching now," I said softly, warning him. He nodded. Though the water was fresh, no steam rose. He didn't heat the water, and I wondered why.

Lorik gave no indication that he even felt the needle piercing into him. I made quick work of it, and only when he had a fresh bandage on his clean skin did I start to feel more at ease.

Rocking back on my heels, I looked at him.

Lorik turned his head to regard me though he looked like a spoiled prince reclining in the tub.

"Why don't you heat the water?"

"Will you join me if I do?"

A flood of heat burned in my belly. "Don't be silly."

"I'm being infinitely serious," he replied, straight-faced, no hint of amusement on his features.

I tucked a strand of loose, wavy hair behind my ear, wetting my suddenly dry lips. My hands needed to be washed, but I couldn't move. Not when he was looking at me the way he was.

Lorik took pity on me. He smiled. Whatever mask he'd had in place before vanished...or perhaps his grinning, handsome face was more of a mask than I realized.

"I don't heat the water because it's a comfort. And I don't need comfort right now. I need to remember."

"Remember what?" I whispered.

"My duty," he murmured, lowering his chin before jutting it forward, gesturing toward the front room of my cottage, to the door. "To protect."

My brow furrowed. "From...from the Severs?"

"He wasn't a Sever," Lorik snapped. While his tone wasn't harsh, I still felt the bite of his words. "He was a Shade. A murderer. A thief. An oath breaker. And he wanted to die. He knew I would end him. I gave him mercy when I should have let him rot into this forest."

"What?" I whispered. I'd always known that there was more to Lorik than I could see...but this? "A Shade?"

"A Shade is what the Allavari *think* Severs are," he said, rolling his good shoulder, bringing a hand up to pinch between his brows. Then he inspected underneath his short claws, flicked out a piece of dried blood, and then took up the cloth again, scrubbing around his fingers. "But Severs have their own laws. Shades break them. Some were cast out from the Below, to be hunted or to be alone."

"How...how do you know all this?" I asked, my heart thrumming in my throat.

Lorik met my eyes. Bright, swirling blue. For a long while, he said nothing. Then...

"In Olimara, there's a collection of three books in the library," he said, his gaze sliding away, scrubbing at his claws again.

"Olimara?" I asked. "The western village on the other side of the Black Veil?"

He inclined his head once. "Books rumored to have been stolen from the Below. By a Sever. Brought up to the Above world and given in exchange for the right to live in the village, to live out the rest of his days there."

"And is that true?" I asked, utterly still. I'd never been to Olimara. Was that where Lorik lived?

"Who knows," Lorik said, his tone gruff. "Everyone lies."

"Even you?" I asked before I thought better of it.

"*Especially* me," he said, his sharp smile returning.

The flash of his fangs made me jolt, made me remember that it was nightfall and he likely needed to feed, especially after expending that energy on the Sever. Or…the Shade.

"You've killed Shades before," I commented.

"Only ones that get too close to the villages," he told me. "Or the ones who want to die."

"You give them mercy even though you don't think you should?" I asked, my gaze sliding down the line of his slick chest before I could stop myself. "Why?"

"It's only more pain and suffering," he replied. "Better to end it. Pain has power. It has energy, like magic. Why allow it to spread? Why not twist off its head right where it stands?"

There was something rising in me at the brutal edge of his words. Something I didn't understand.

Lorik cocked his head. Water trickled when he raised an arm, and I felt his hand clasp my chin, his thumb stroking the bottom of my lip.

"Do you like that, my bloodthirsty little witch?"

"I'm not bloodthirsty," I whispered, unable to look away.

"You like it when I'm cruel though. Or merciful—however

you wish to look at it," he replied. His eyes were glowing again. They were all I could see.

"I like it when you don't hesitate," I corrected, the words falling out of me in a rush. My lip was wet from his thumb, and he stroked over the flesh. Unconsciously, I darted my tongue out to catch the water, and he made a sound in the back of his throat when it met the roughened pad of his thumb.

"Explain," he ordered, his gaze on my lips, like he wished I would lick him again.

"When you...when you don't overthink *anything*. You act. Some might call it unpredictable, but I don't think it's that at all," I confessed softly, my throat tight with want and desire and something that felt strangely like panic. "I think you know yourself better than most people know themselves. Your morality, your values, your lies, and your truths. I think you see the world ten steps ahead of everyone else."

"Then why didn't I ask you to Grimstone's and steal your kiss in a back booth if you believe I don't hesitate when it comes to what I want?" he questioned.

"I didn't say that. I didn't say only when it comes to what *you* want. But I think you know why you haven't asked me to Grimstone's," I whispered. "I don't. But you do. There's a reason for it —one I cannot see yet."

"But are you beginning to see it?" he questioned, leaning forward, his chest pressing harder against the side of the washing tub. "Are you beginning to see who I am, little witch?"

"I'm not even close," I admitted, my eyes half-lidded, leaning toward him. "I know your name is Lorik Ravael. I know you don't live in Rolara. I know Veras knows you and he thinks you're dangerous. I know you joke and smile with the lonely old silk trader at the market and that it makes her whole week. I know you watch people, I know you see a lot more than many do. I know you were struck with a poisoned arrow with a metal tip when Allavari only use wood. I know you've killed Severs...only you call them Shades. And that you've read books in Olimara. And that you have a sister who you would do anything for, though I've never seen you with anyone in the village. And I know…"

I swallowed, licking my lips again, and I felt the pressure of Lorik's thumb increase on my bottom lip.

"You know what, Marion?"

"I know that you look at me like you don't look at anyone else. Unless even that's a lie," I couldn't help but add. "Is it?"

"Hmmm. Tell me how I look at you, and I'll tell you if it's a lie," he rasped.

"Like…like you want me. Like I'm the one thing you can't figure out and it drives you mad," I answered honestly, memory of catching his pensive frown on me in the market. "Like you want nothing more than to steal my kiss and for some reason you just won't. Or can't. Like—"

Lorik leaned forward, his movements so quick they were a blur.

His palm spread over my cheek, his long fingers extending toward the nape of my neck, tugging me toward him.

His lips were warm and soft…but his kiss was firm.

I gasped, my scalp tingling, a full-body shiver racking me.

"Not a lie," he whispered against my lips. His tongue lapped at mine, his fangs brushing my bottom lip, teasing. "How's this for not hesitating?"

CHAPTER 13

His husky words drifted over my tongue, threading down my throat, until it felt like I'd consumed them entirely.

He hadn't hesitated—not this time—and so I didn't either. And maybe it was the emotion of the afternoon and evening—Veras and the Sever and the dark look in Lorik's eyes when he'd spoken of mercy and Shades—but I needed *something*. I needed an escape. An outlet.

And I knew I would find it in Lorik.

Our kiss grew to be a desperate thing, roving and seeking like a moon wolf scenting prey. His hot breath drifted between my lips. I inhaled his scent like bonfire smoke, making me dizzy, making the walls spin. His kiss made my mouth tingle, like I could feel the pinpricks of his magic trailing along my skin, pleasant little zings that only made me demand more.

My hands went to his wet shoulders. I forgot about his wound, but he didn't even flinch when I accidentally hit the bandage.

"Lorik," I gasped out, feeling need rise in me, growing and growing to new heights that it was almost frightening. There was a buzzing underneath my skin, one that made me so full of energy I thought I might burst. Especially if he didn't touch me the way I wanted.

It had been much too long since I'd slept with a man. Since I'd felt the weight and heat and press of one. Since I'd felt whispered sighs drift across my skin and felt the sweat cooling on my chest in the afterglow.

I'd hidden myself away in the Black Veil in my grief…but it had been ten years and I'd been paralyzed here. Unable to move forward.

I didn't want that anymore. And I had a Kylorr-Allavari male, who was much more than he seemed, pressed into me.

And I wanted him.

I wanted him so desperately I thought I would choke on my need.

Lorik, thank the gods, seemed to feel that same desperation clawing inside him because he stood from the washing tub in one swift motion. He broke our kiss only momentarily, and I stared up at him with a half-lidded gaze, lips swollen and red, as I kneeled in front of him.

Despite the icy water he'd been bathing in, and despite the fact that I'd just stitched up a wound—a wound that he'd only recently recovered from, his cock was as hard as Allavari steel.

"One chance," he told me, the words drenched in warning though they fell from his lips like a purr. "One chance to leave, little witch. Because if I have you tonight, there's no going back."

Maybe if I wasn't panting like a dog in heat, maybe if he hadn't kissed me until I couldn't even recall my own name I might've answered differently. I might've paused, given his words honest and deliberate thought.

But instead, I reached up, and the shocking heat of his hard cock met my palm. I gripped him tightly, finally eliciting a hiss and a whispered curse from him, his hips bucking forward. I traced the length of one thick vein up the shaft, but I didn't make it to the tip.

Before I knew it, Lorik had darted from the washing tub and I was up in his arms before I could blink. The chill of his icy flesh made me gasp, but he swallowed it down with another stolen kiss, one that made me cling to his shoulders—though I was mindful of his bandaged wound this time.

"Patience, little witch," he groaned, squeezing my backside with one large palm as he strode from the washroom. "I intend to savor this."

His words brought about wicked fantasies that streamed into my head on a loop. But most of all, I wanted to touch him and explore every little thing that drove him wild. I wanted to make him come undone. I wanted to see Lorik Ravael ripped apart at the seams. Maybe then I could finally discover the secrets he was hiding. Who he truly was.

When my back met the warm sheets of my bed, I realized Lorik must've finished washing them for me when I'd been… otherwise occupied at Aysia's grave.

That realization alone made me deepen his kiss as his weight came down on top of me, pinning me to the bed. His wings covered us like a blanket, spreading out so that they blocked the light coming in from the front room. Those tiny little membranes in his wings fascinated me, and I wanted to trace every little vein there like I'd traced the one lining his cock.

I saw blood bloom under the fresh bandage, given that he was hovering off me with his strength.

"Lorik," I gasped.

"Leave it," he growled, distracting me as he nearly ripped the front half of my dress down my own arms, trapping them at my sides though it bared my breasts to him. His eyes glowed brighter at the sight until we were lit with a soft cast of blue. "It'll heal."

I was torn between desire and duty…at least until Lorik dropped his head and I felt the heat of his mouth envelope my breast. I heard the whistle of his hitched breath against my skin, almost contented as he licked and laved.

"Oh gods," I breathed, widening my thighs so he could sink further into me, melting against him until I felt boneless. He captured my nipple between his teeth, making me hold my breath, the tip of his fang a dangerous tease. With my nipple tight in his grasp, he stroked the underside with his tongue, and I moaned throatily. The perfect mix of pleasure and pain. "Lorik!"

Even still, I caught the fresh scent of his blood, and I groaned.

"Lorik, your—"

A rough sound left his throat though it was followed by a husky, languid chuckle, one that felt like silk skimming my skin.

"Heal me, then, little witch," he purred. "And I know exactly what I need."

With that he rolled off me, going to his back on the bed. I was relieved when the weight was off his shoulder at the very least.

"Stand up," he ordered.

I swallowed, feeling the cool air drift over my breast where he'd suckled, puckering the sensitive flesh and making me *burn*. I stood from the bed.

"That's my good little witch," he praised. "Now, take off your dress."

"I should get the needle and—"

"Take off your dress. *Now.*"

The edge in his tone had me wiggling from the material, suddenly desperate to hear what he'd order me to do next. Had my two past lovers ever dared to order me around when it came to sex? No.

A pity, I realized, feeling something unlock in me. Something I wanted to explore.

When I was naked, my dress pooled at my feet and the end of

my hair tickling the edge of one nipple, Lorik's gaze trailed up my body slowly. *Savoring,* I realized.

It was so quiet, I wondered if Lorik could hear my heart throbbing in my chest. With impatience. With need. With nerves. It had been so long, what if I'd forgotten how to be someone?

"You're an incredibly beautiful woman, Marion," came his words. Soft and gentle.

"You think so?" I asked, a smile pulling at my lips. My belly fluttered. Lorik might've been a liar, like he'd proclaimed, but all I'd heard was soft honesty—even *reverence*—in his tone.

"Gods, yes," he groaned. "Come here."

"How is this healing you?" I asked again, stepping toward the bed, eyeing his bandage.

"You'll see," he rasped, watching me place a knee on the edge of the firm mattress. "No, come up here. I need a taste of you."

Heat burned my cheeks, but I was much too curious and eager to protest.

"Like this?" I asked, my tone pitched high, when I settled my knees around his face, careful of his shoulder and his wings. And his horns, but that was more for my sake, I knew as I eyed the sharpened tips.

"Perfect," he whispered, and I let out a deep sigh when I felt that word drift between my thighs. Lorik's arms came around my hips, holding me down. "I want you to let go."

When the wet heat of his tongue registered against my pussy, I gasped. I didn't know what he'd meant by those last words until my thighs began to shake and I realized he wanted me to *let go*. To *give in* to every sensation and every lick and lap and every tease that inched me closer and closer to the edge of pleasure.

"Lorik," I moaned. The grip on my hips tightened with his name, and I reached back to steady myself on his chest so I didn't fall right over. But the position only opened me up to him more.

His tongue felt like it was everywhere all at once. Hot and

slick and delicious and wicked. The muscles in my legs were trembling. The moans tumbling from my lips seemed to fill the air until I could hear nothing else.

Right when I was on the edge of an orgasm, Lorik pulled back.

"No!" I cried out, my eyes flying open.

He grinned between my thighs, those eyes practically as feral as that smile. His lips were shining with my slickness, but I couldn't find it in me to be embarrassed.

"Greedy little witch," he said. His voice was unrecognizable, deep and rough with his desire. The edge of his finger teased at my opening when he moved it from my hip. I bucked against his hand, desperate to be filled by something. *Anything.*

When he thrust a finger into me, my lips parted and my head lolled around my shoulders. His thumb pressed against my clit, but the thickness of his finger inside me felt even more perfect.

But then...I felt his fangs skim my inner thigh. I gasped and looked down. Only when I met his eyes, realization making mine widen in anticipation, did he bite down.

Healing him, came the wild thought. This was what he'd meant.

The prick of his fangs registered as his venom flooded the small wound. Whatever chemistry we had, whatever reason—whether divine fate or magic or mere biology—that made his bite feel orgasmic, I didn't question it. I only enjoyed it.

Lorik groaned, deep in his throat in between his pulling draws of my blood.

Every suck made my eyes roll. He'd had me on the edge of orgasm already with his tongue and his touch. This? It felt like I *could* come merely from this.

"Lorik," I groaned, his name edged with panic and pleasure. I was frightened of how good it might feel to come like this, but I thought I'd never be the same if I didn't experience it.

He dislodged his fangs briefly, and I nearly cried with frustration.

"Look at me," he purred, wedging another finger deep, joining the first and making me shiver. "Look over your shoulder and see what you do to me, Marion. See how hard you make my cock. See how much I fucking *ache* for you."

Right when I did what he ordered, I felt him bite down again.

My lips parted when I saw his cock. Thick and hard and bobbing with need. A pool of pre-come had settled into the rigid lines of muscles lining his abdomen. The veins were even more prominent, and I wanted to lick every last one.

Gods, the sight of him like that was sexy. So incredibly arousing. I wanted to lap at his shimmering, silvery pre-come off his belly and make him moan.

"Mmmm," he hummed against me, no doubt feeling the gush of slickness between my thighs at the sight.

"I love that," I breathed, greedy for him. Reaching back, I took his cock in my hand, so hot it felt like it could burn me if I wasn't careful. So hot that for a moment I feared his fever might've returned if not for the coolness of his skin beneath me. "I love that I make you like this."

He groaned when I stroked him, his deep draws of my blood even more pronounced, and my thighs tightened around his face. My body was beginning to shake, the sublime pleasure from his feeding nearly overwhelming.

Let go, I remembered.

I let out a choking gasp, my hand tightening around his thick, perfect cock as I began to orgasm.

Lorik felt the change, felt me clamping down on his fingers like a vise as I cried out and bucked. His other arm held me steadily in place, his other hand working between my thighs.

And he never stopped his feeding.

"Oh gods," I choked, the air in my lungs being tugged from

me as if it could be tethered to a rope and pulled. My belly contracted, my moans filled the air as the best orgasm of my entire damn life unleashed in me. The outlet I'd needed. The *relief.*

I'd known Lorik would give it to me, hadn't I?

When it was over, Lorik was continuing to feed. I kept a grip on his cock, feeling him buck his hips into my grip like he was imagining fucking me, and when I met his eyes, they were *burning* into mine.

Even in the aftermath of the orgasm, I could feel him already beginning to stoke the remaining embers.

He wasn't done with me, I realized.

I intend to savor this, he'd told me.

The night was far from over.

CHAPTER 14

Lorik released his fangs from me, but he didn't heal the wound.

"I want to see my mark on you," he rasped, retracting his fingers from my still-clenching pussy and using the wetness to brush my sensitive clit. I sucked in a sharp breath. "Beautiful."

He had me in his grip before I could say a word, effortlessly lifting my boneless body off him until I found myself lying sideways across the bed. Lorik stood, looming over me in the darkness, taking his cock in his hand. I licked my lips, watching as he gave it a few steady pumps, squeezing tight around the thick, bulbous head.

"This is what you want, Marion?" he questioned, voice guttural and low. He stepped closer, between my splayed thighs, kneeling slightly so that he could run the head of his cock over the sensitive, hot flesh.

I whimpered, biting my lip.

"Tell me," he ordered.

"Yes," I breathed.

He smirked. "Yes…what?"

Maddening male, I thought.

I arched my back so we pressed together again, and he let out a low groan.

"Yes, I want your cock."

"Good," he whispered, his eyes appearing to burn brighter. I knew he was something different. So why wasn't I afraid of him? Even when I caught ripples of magic over his skin, even when I'd felt his magic in his kiss, why hadn't I been afraid then?

That gaze roved down my body, drinking me in. He reached forward to pinch one of my nipples gently, just as the heat of his cock met my entrance. He used it to tease me, and even on the heels of that incredible orgasm, I found myself tensing with anticipation and impatience.

"I wanted this to be slow," he told him, sinking into me a couple inches, making me gasp. "I wanted to take my time with you, but I don't know if I can."

"I don't want you to take your time," I said, the tone of my voice practically a whine. I pushed myself up onto my elbows to get a better view, and Lorik's hand cupped my breast fully. "Lorik, *please*!"

"Oh, I like that," he purred, sinking into me a few more inches. I felt the burning stretch. He was incredibly—for lack of a better word—*huge*. And it had been a long time for me. "You begging."

Maybe slow is better, I couldn't help but think, huffing as I forced my muscles to relax to take more of him.

"Don't get used to it," I shot back. Lorik let out a husky laugh before he seemed to hold his breath, sliding deeper…and deeper.

Gods, how big was he?

Finally, there was nowhere else for him to go, and I looked up at him with parted lips and half-lidded eyes.

Blood was seeping through the bandage already, but I would take care of him later. He came down on top of me, the heat of his body and the delicious weight of him pressing me into the mattress. He stole another kiss, passionate and almost possessive, as he was seated deep inside me, giving me a moment to get used to his size.

"Mmm, I'm high on your blood and your pussy, my beautiful little witch. There's nothing better than the way you make me feel," he whispered against my lips. His naughty words stoked the fire burning inside my belly, and he groaned when I squeezed around his cock. "Fuck, you feel so good, Marion."

"Lorik," I pleaded.

"You want to come again?"

"Yes!"

Another chuckle that lit my blood on fire. "Very well."

The first hard thrust had me crying out, the room swaying with the overwhelming sensation of delicious friction and pleasure. The second had me scrambling for his shoulders, trying to keep myself in place as the strength of him nearly flung me off the bed. The third and fourth and fifth thrusts had me moaning out his name, digging my fingernails into his back.

Nothing felt as good as him inside me. I understood what he'd meant before.

Our lips met in the chaos of our lovemaking. Warm and comforting, the kiss anchored me to him, my beacon in the storm. Lorik was needful. Strong. Incredibly so. Part Kylorr—I could feel that infamous strength buzzing under his skin. I knew he was holding himself back in fear of hurting me…but I wanted him to give it all to me. His aggression, his desire.

"Let go," I said against his lips, repeating the words he'd said to me. "Let go for me, Lorik."

He groaned, the sound pulled from him harshly. His breathing was labored, both our chests damp from perspiration, and the sounds of our bodies meeting filled the room with an erotic, arousing beat. Like music.

I could feel when he gave himself to me fully. Every measured thrust nearly stole my breath, but I relished the ferocity of him, the wildness.

"Made for me," he growled.

I clenched around him, the pressure from his pelvis stimulating my clit. And the fact that he felt too good inside me. His cock. His voice. His words. I was going to come again…but I wanted him to follow me.

"Close," I gasped out. "Don't stop."

His pace quickened. Even though I didn't think it possible, he slid even deeper, filling me to the brim, more full than I'd ever been before.

His head dropped, and I tilted my head back to avoid his horns, the tip of one brushing my jaw. His lips found my breast. I thought he was going to suck on my nipple again, maybe take it between his teeth. Until…

"Oh gods," I choked out, feeling his fangs slide deeply into the upper flesh. He began to *feed*. "Lorik, I'm going to—"

My orgasm came at me quickly and suddenly. The sucking pull of his feeding, the wicked pleasure and unexpectedness of it, hurtled me off the edge, and I cried out with a breathless gasp, my back arching off the bed, all the muscles in my legs and abdomen tightening.

"Fuuuck," came his muttered curse, though it was muffled against me. He groaned, no doubt feeling me clamp down on him, his pace quickening, hips jerking against me in a chaotic rhythm.

Through the ringing in my ears, I heard his almost anguished moan, low and deep. When I opened my heavy eyelids, I saw his head was flung back, his long hair tangling in his horns. With his eyes screwed shut, I witnessed the beautiful pleasure cross his features just as I felt the heat of his come shoot into me, the ragged buck of his hips as he chased his orgasm down.

A veil appeared to shimmer over his face. For a moment, Lorik's features appeared sharper yet somehow broader. His body seemed to grow around me, but my hands remained in place.

When I blinked, whatever image I'd witnessed was gone. Lorik's eyes caught mine, and he leaned down to kiss me.

The orgasms have addled my brain, I thought, dismissing what I'd seen. I closed my eyes, pressing myself into him, and he shuddered, his hips lazily rocking into me as his own climax faded.

In the aftermath, it was quiet. Lorik leaned into me, the heavy bulk of his body comforting. I had my arms wrapped around his neck, clinging to him as the sweat on our skin cooled and our hearts slowed. My fingers met the edge of the bandage on the back of his shoulder, where the metal arrow had pierced through.

He let out a long breath that ruffled my hair.

Into my ear, he murmured, "No going back now, Marion."

CHAPTER 15

The fire in the hearth crackled, and I felt Lorik's hand dip from my hip bone, slowly trailing around my backside, giving a light squeeze.

"Stop," I chided, unable to keep the wide grin that stretched over my features at bay, negating my stern word.

For his sake, Lorik looked repentant, even as he gave my ass another squeeze. "I'm sorry, healer. Forgive me."

I chuckled, feeling a dull ache between my legs when I moved behind him. He was seated on the chair in the front room. And I was fixing his sutures. Yet again. From the feeding, from my blood, he'd already begun to heal, but I didn't want the thread to get trapped under his skin. Even for a Kylorr, he healed remarkably fast. Though I wondered if that had more to do with his Allavari ancestry as well. Likely a combination of both, I finally decided.

"Not too bad," I commented as I finished the last stitch. "The skin is a little ravaged," I admitted. "But it'll heal quickly. I put more salve on it. Try not to jostle it too much."

"Tell that to my new lover—she's demanding," came his

reply, and my face heated at the word. *Lover.* He tsked. "After tonight, you're still shy?"

I squeaked when Lorik tugged me into his lap—his still-naked lap, and I felt the side of his half-hard cock brush my arm. His kiss came suddenly, and I stilled, breathing into it, tingles shooting into my scalp. A kiss so sweet it made my teeth ache.

"And you say I'm the demanding one," I teased gently, pulling back. "I still have a needle in my hand," I warned.

"What's the old Allavari saying? A needle through eye if you're not spry?"

I huffed out a breath and slapped at his hand when it began to wander. I grinned as I escaped his grip, smoothing my hair and my dress. Crossing to my cabinets, I used the time to get my heart under control. I dropped my tools into a soaking dish to sanitize and wrapped the remainder of the clean bandages neatly, tucking them into a lined drawer.

"I'm going to have to go into the market to get you more bandages at this rate," I noted. For the bloodied ones, I tossed those into a basket to be burned with purple fire.

"I'll go with you. We could go to Grimstone's Tavern," he said.

I sighed.

"Wouldn't you like that?" he asked, leaning back in the chair, the tops of his wings twitching. I studied him like this, thinking it a shame that I didn't have Aysia's talent for art. Because I would've loved to capture this moment with paper and ink. To draw him just like this, frozen in time and in memory.

And Lorik would be a perfect subject. All sharp bones and maddeningly handsome features. He'd always made Rolara's population of females swoon, even though none dared to approach him. He just had…an energy about him that warned others away.

Prey instinct, I thought. And most could sense that he was the predator. Or something like one. Dangerous. He was calculated while giving the impression that he was unpredictable.

"What are you thinking?" Lorik wondered, cocking his head to the side. "I can see the thoughts churning in that mind of yours."

"Have you always had magic stronger than other Allavari?" I questioned, not wanting to tell him the entire truth.

"This again?" he rasped. "I told you before. I just know how to wield it more efficiently than most."

"And who taught you that?"

He smiled. "Myself."

"There was a moment in there," I said, nodding my head to the door to my bedroom, "toward the end where it looked like you were someone else."

Lorik blinked, lowering his chin. "How so?"

I shrugged a shoulder but kept it lifted, crossing my arms over my chest. "It was you, but it looked like there was magic shimmering over your face. You looked different. Stronger. Your features appeared more…sharp."

If anything, he'd been even more beautiful, and I already didn't think his beauty was fair. Allavari were known to be a physically beautiful race, with their willowy, graceful bodies and perfect symmetry.

Throw in Kylorr genes?

There might be such a thing as being *too* handsome, and Lorik already toed that line.

"What are you asking me?" Lorik wondered quietly, eyeing me.

"Does…does that happen to Kylorr males a lot?"

Lorik blew out a short breath. I had the impression he was thinking about his answer with deliberateness.

"Kylorr get stronger during sex and especially after release. Though sex tempers our berserker rages, sex is still a primal thing. It calls to our baser instincts. It will always bring out aggression for a Kylorr. Satisfying aggression. And feeding during sex? It guarantees there will be a physical response. That's likely what you saw."

I swallowed past the thick lump in my throat. "I…I thought that might be the case. For living on a planet whose population is part Kylorr, I know embarrassingly little about them."

"You're a healer," Lorik pointed out, gesturing me forward when he noticed I was lingering on the edge of his reach. I stepped into him, and he widened his legs, taking my palms in his. "Shouldn't you study Kylorr to know them better?"

"I should," I admitted. "But Kylorr get injured very rarely. And most that do heal quickly. Besides…I…I haven't exactly been involved in village life. No one wants to trek all the way out here to be seen by me. The ones that do…they need the remedies only I have."

"From your glowflies," Lorik said.

"Yes."

"The shadevines," he guessed.

"Yes," I said. "But the people I see have usually been poisoned or have some kind of rare infection that's taken hold. Tending to flesh wounds…I haven't done that in a long time."

"You tell me that now?" Lorik teased.

"You were poisoned, had an infection, *and* had a difficult flesh wound," I pointed out. "I think I did pretty damn well, considering the circumstances."

Lorik chuckled, running his hands up my sides until they clasped my waist. He leaned forward, pressing a kiss to the middle of my abdomen. Against the thin dress I'd thrown on after our lovemaking, I could hear him murmur, "You did a wonderful job, my little witch."

His praise made me want to sink into a puddle at his feet.

"How are you feeling?" Lorik asked.

"About?"

"Much has happened today," he commented. "Did you expect any of it?"

Veras. Aysia. The Sev—the Shade. And what had happened between us afterward. That was what he meant.

"No," I admitted. "I don't make it a habit to sleep with my patients."

"You better not," he grumbled, and I settled my hand on his warm chest, feeling so protected and safe in his lap. "You know what I mean."

I sighed. "It's been a long day—you're right."

"Are you tired?"

"Surprisingly, no."

"Good. Me neither," he said.

"You should rest, Lorik," I said. "Your infection was just—"

"I'm fine, Marion," he told me. "I told you before. I'm stronger than I look. This wound will be gone by the end of the week, if not sooner, and it'll be like it never happened."

And then he'll be gone, I thought, a surprising wave of loneliness crashing down into me. There was no reason for him to stay. Now that the poison was out of his system and he'd already overcome the lingering infection, come morning, he would have no reason to be here.

"Then I'll only see you at market days," I couldn't help but whisper.

Lorik's arm tightened around my back, and he dragged his hand over my hip. "Is that what you want? Only on market days?"

Sucking in a sharp breath, I met his eyes. There was a sullenness in his tone, one that matched mine perfectly. "No, I don't want that. Not only on market days. But I've never seen you in Rolara on other days. You're like a ghost."

"So are you," he replied. But he didn't tell me where he lived. He said nothing else about it. "Can I ask you something personal?"

"Do you need permission?" I teased, hiding my disappointment.

"I suppose I could ask anyway and you could just tell me to fuck off," he murmured.

"Yes, always a possibility," I said, the edge of my lips curling before I sobered. "Ask."

"Aysia," Lorik said, and I tensed slightly. "Maybe it's not so much a question. More of…I want to know you. I want to know everything about you, and she was a large part of your life. I've heard things in the village, idle gossip. I want to hear it from you."

I nodded, swallowing. I pushed off his lap and went to my counter, filling a kettle with fresh water from the tap.

"Tea?" I asked.

"Sure." His tone was at ease, relaxed, like we'd done this a million times. I knew he could sense I wasn't running away, but I just needed to speak about Aysia in my own way.

I plopped the kettle on the hook over the fire in the hearth and added another log, sparks flying. Straightening, I looked down into the flames and crossed my arms over my chest as I waited for it to boil.

"Correl's orphanage, as I'm sure you know, was not a wonderful place to grow up," I told him.

"I've heard the stories. It burned down, didn't it? Correl died in the fire," Lorik said.

"That would have been Veras's handiwork," I confessed. "Though he'll never admit it. He did it for Aysia, in his own twisted way. I think a part of her even liked it. Anyway…I grew up with a woman—an Allavari woman—who had taken me in since I was a baby. I never knew my parents. She was kind to me —at least I think so. I only have fond memories of her. But she died when I was seven, and I went to live at the orphanage. I was there about a year before Aysia came. She was so small then. Just a child."

Lorik frowned. "You raised her?"

I nodded. "I was a mother and a sister to her. Maybe that's why I find it so hard to move on. To forgive. Because I *raised* her and I was no more than a child myself."

Lorik cursed under his breath, soft and gentle.

"I was the eldest at Correl's. I took care of many children, but with Aysia...our bond was always different. It was special. The others knew it. They would pick on her and I did what I could to protect her...but children can be cruel. She was alone a lot even though she had me. Correl would beat her with this strap when she didn't come back by curfew. I would tend to her wounds, try to make her feel better."

My throat tightened. After today, this was likely the last thing I wanted to talk about, but it felt good in its own way. Like picking off a scab that itched.

"We got older. We had all these plans. I would pledge myself to the Healers' Guild when I was of age. I would take her when I left Correl's, and she would apprentice under an artist so she could eventually pledge herself to the Artists' Guild. But we would live together in a little cottage and have a home all our own where no one could hurt us again. And we would be free."

The water in the kettle began to steam, and I took it from its holder, being careful not to burn myself. When I turned, I saw that Lorik had stood from his chair, a restless energy about him. He caught my wrist when I passed and took the kettle.

"Sit down," he told me. Then he went to the cabinets, pulling out cups and silk satchels of dried tea leaves after I watched him rummage with endless curiosity. "Go on."

He made us tea—naked in my kitchen—while I sunk down on the opposite chair, my back to the fire. Peek, I noticed, was sleeping, curled under the bench by the front door. Maybe he'd finally decided he trusted Lorik. His ears were relaxed, no longer perked, even in his slumber.

"And that's what almost happened," I continued, sighing,

sliding my arms across the table, sweeping away unseen dust and playing with the edge of a thread I'd trimmed away from the spool. "I came of age. I left and took Aysia with me. I pledged myself to the Healers' Guild, taking work where I could while studying beside them. Aysia got an apprenticeship. A few years later, Aysia came of age. And right when she was about to make her pledge…she met Veras. Then everything changed."

"In what ways?" Lorik wondered, coming to the table with two mugfuls of steaming tea. The bitterness of the leaves perfumed the air, and I watched as he sat down in the opposite chair, sliding my cup across the wood table. His hand strayed close to my own, and he gave it a gentle caress, fluttering my belly, before pulling away. He leaned back in his chair, all warm, muscled flesh and a quizzical frown.

"I hardly ever saw her, for one," I answered. "I think a part of me was jealous. He swept her off her feet, gave her anything she wanted. Their courtship was fast. Within a week of meeting, she was basically living with him on his estate. She stopped training under her artist, she decided to forgo the pledges for that particular year for the guild. All she talked about was Veras. She was in love. They both were," I conceded.

"When did it start to go bad?"

"A few months in," I replied, swallowing, wrapping my hand around the hot cup. "Everyone knew about Veras Lain. His illegal dealings with off-planet merchants for Allavari weapons."

"Among other things," Lorik commented, raising a brow.

"Exactly," I said quietly. "Every time I tried to warn her or…" I sighed. "It only pushed her further away. We had a big fight about him a few months into their courtship, and she didn't speak to me for almost four months. And when we finally reconciled…we were both so relieved, I think, to be back in one another's lives that we played pretend. We didn't speak about Veras, but she always went home to him. She always turned a blind eye to what he did. She gave up her art. Her entire life became him.

And for the most part, I think she was happy with him. He made her happy, but…it cost her a lot. Too much."

"Her life," Lorik said gently, reaching across the table to take my hand. My heart gave a little throb at the gesture, and I threaded my fingers with his.

"Yes," I whispered. "It happened so suddenly. Veras was meeting with a group of mercenaries from Jetutia. The negotiations turned bad apparently. They got angry. And Aysia…Aysia was there at the wrong time. They took her, ransomed her. Veras gave them the weapons they wanted…and they still killed her to punish him."

"Fuck," Lorik rasped, and my vision went blurry with that word. The days she'd been missing…they'd been absolute hell. "Marion, I'm sorry."

I took a sip of my bitter tea, steeped a little too long, but I found the bite just distracting enough.

"It was nearly ten years ago now, and some days, it feels like it just happened," I admitted. "And I was numb for a really long time. Then I was angry. And now…I don't know *what* I am anymore."

Lorik's gaze softened. "You're breaking my heart, little witch."

"But Veras might be right. I told you earlier. I just can't…I can't do this anymore. This isn't the life I want."

"Being alone?" he asked.

A small, sad smile curled my lips. "Yes, that, but I feel like I'm just waiting for something. Or just wasting time. I can never be sure which. Do you ever feel that way?"

"I think everyone has felt that way at one point in their life," he said.

"When did you?" I challenged.

He blew out a sharp breath, leaning forward in his chair even as his thumb stroked the back of my hand.

"Maybe right now," he answered. "Can I speak freely without you asking too many questions?"

It was better than nothing, I decided. And I thought he figured I was smart enough to know that he was being secretive about something he couldn't say.

I nodded.

"I feel like I'm at a crossroads, being pulled in two different directions, by two entirely different places. I was raised with a purpose. There is a comfort in that. A familiarity. But I am also curious. About many things. Places, people, history. In choosing one, I cannot have the other. In choosing the other…I fear it will cost me more than I'm willing to pay. I don't want to turn my back on my duty, to my family, to my *people*."

Lorik squeezed my hand, giving me a slight smile.

"I think we are in similar positions, Marion," he told me. "Don't you think?"

"Yes, just without the legacy aspect, I suppose," I murmured, noticing that he was trying to lighten the mood. It had settled too deep, and after the weight of the day, it was beginning to feel too heavy.

"We should figure it out together."

My breath nearly whooshed out of my lungs at the pronouncement.

"I'm being serious," he said, eyeing me, that smile having never left. "Are we in agreement?"

"I've always heard you shouldn't make bargains with an Allavari. Because you'll likely lose more than you think," I said, if only to buy time.

His teeth flashed, the tips of his fangs poking into his bottom lip, making me remember the wound between my thighs where he'd bitten me as I'd orgasmed.

"Good thing I'm part Kylorr and the berserker in me would keep to its honor," he replied, as quick as ever.

I laughed. It felt good, like a release…when I'd already had a couple tonight, I remembered with heated cheeks. Lorik looked at me over the rim of his cup as he sipped on his tea.

"Can't argue with that," I finally said. Almost shyly, I added, "All right, it's a deal."

"Good," Lorik replied, the word sharp and clear. His gaze studied my face, those eyes observing at his leisure. "Thank you for telling me about Aysia."

I nodded, observing him just like he was observing me.

"You have a beautiful soul, Marion," he murmured. He'd said something like that before, and it still made my heart leap. "You would make anyone very happy."

"Thank you," I said, trying to fight the flustered beam that threatened to break out over my face. It was like I was swinging on emotions with him…but he made me feel safe. *Heard.* I felt like he did truly want to know everything about me because he cared about me. Because he knew that maybe one day, we would be *more* to one another.

"Too bad I'm a greedy bastard and I want you all to myself. The others can wait in line," he deadpanned.

The laugh that sounded was louder than the first.

"Stop," I whispered.

"No," he answered, a small smile playing over his lips as he watched me. I had the impression he was drinking me in. *Really* looking at me. "Are you sore from earlier?"

"No," I said softly. I *was*, actually, a little sore, but I wouldn't admit it because I wanted him again too.

"Good," he rasped, standing from the table, rounding toward me with that commanding body. "Now that I have you, I intend to take complete advantage."

"Oh, really?" I asked, quirking a brow.

"Absolutely," he said. "Don't say I didn't warn you, little witch."

CHAPTER 16

The following night, we were in the garden.

Lorik's hand strayed below my waist, and I shot him a stern look, which had his lips twitching. The glowflies illuminated his face in varying shades of color as they bobbed and weaved and worked around us. The glowflies liked Lorik—or at least the brightbells and the death needle varieties did. The fire cups? Not so much. The shadevines…he'd nearly been stung.

One death needle glowfly landed on the tip of his horn, illuminating the striations of the black bone in silver light. I chuckled and said, "You look cute with your little friend."

The look in Lorik's eyes as he watched me nearly had me melting in place. Warm and gentle, it made my heart thud rapidly in my chest.

He likes me, I thought, the knowledge filling me with dizzy hope and excitement. *He likes me a lot.*

Lorik reached up, and the glowfly crawled onto the outstretched tip of his claw. He brought it down with care, observing the small insect, taking in its transparent, large wings and the way its body shimmered like a jewel.

"Most people are afraid of death needles because of their

name," I commented softly, observing them both. Behind him, I saw Peek in the hollow of the tree, spying in the garden, one of his favorite nooks outside. I smiled. "But they are actually the gentlest and most harmless of all the glowflies. Wrathweeds... those are the ones you need to watch out for."

"I'll stay all the way over here with you, then," Lorik rumbled. "Marvelous little things, aren't they? With more magic in their bodies than most Allavari possess in their lifetime."

"Do you think it's true?" I wondered. "What the villages are saying? That the Below is somehow leeching magic from this land? That Allavari are losing their power because of it?"

Lorik's gaze met mine. The death needle glowfly flitted from his claw, landing on the nearby plant I was tending to, and out of the corner of my eye, I saw the tiny insect burrow its way into the blackness of the flower.

"No, I don't think that's true," he replied.

"Do you think the Allavari are losing their magic?"

"I think that the Allavari like to blame others for their problems and lack of dedication and study to their craft," Lorik said. "Magic is an element. It's like the air we breathe, the soil in the earth. Nothing more. To strengthen and hone it, it takes practice and care. Focus and study. It's a spiritual thing. It's not supposed to come easily. The Allavari have simply forgotten that."

"Do they have a 'Study of Magic' Guild in Olimara?" I teased, clearing out a stray weed from the death needle bed, tossing it to the ground.

"Olimara?" he questioned. "Why Olimara?"

"Because I figured you're the head of that guild, if there was such one. And since you don't live in Rolara, I thought maybe you lived in Olimara since you mentioned it before."

"I don't have only one home," he replied, picking up the weed I'd plucked, twirling it around in his fingers. "I have many. I like it that way."

"So you're like a nomad, flitting from village to village?" I asked.

His lips curled, and he shot me a sharp look. "Something like that."

Did he know I was trying to pry? But he was so private and closed off about anything personal that I was beginning to feel strangely about it.

"I don't know much about you, Lorik," I said softly. "For all I know, you could have a mate tucked away somewhere with five or six children running around and I would be none the wiser."

Lorik narrowed his eyes. "Do you believe I'm that type of male?"

"No," I said. "But you never truly know someone, isn't that right? I, um, was involved with a male from the village…oh, six years ago, maybe? He told me all sorts of things, promised all sorts of things. Turns out he was a liar and he stole all my potions on his way out. So…my instincts about someone have been wrong before."

A strained silence followed. Truthfully, I was a little embarrassed to have admitted that I'd been taken advantage of by a man I'd trusted. Umerie had been his name. He'd had beautiful silver eyes and a charming smile. And I might've been too lonely and desperate to feel *anything* that I'd been blinded by him. I didn't want that to happen again.

"Marion," Lorik said. Hesitantly, I looked up to meet his eyes. "I can promise you with every part of me that I don't have a mate or children hidden somewhere. You're the only woman I want, the only one I've even allowed myself to get close to in a long time. That's something you never have to worry about with me."

I nodded, turning back to the garden bed. His words burned in my belly and brought heat to my cheeks. I was glad it was a chilly night to help hide it, but I had a feeling that Lorik knew the effect of his words anyway.

"You're...you're the only male I've allowed myself to get close to in a long time too," I confessed.

"Let me show you something," he murmured. Curious, I turned back to him, and he took my hand, placing the stem of the weed between my fingertips.

I held it, and he closed his palm around mine. I savored his heat and the calloused brush of his fingers.

"You have more magic than you think—I've told you before," he murmured, staring down at our joined hands. "And when I join yours with mine..."

I gasped, feeling that familiar tingle crawl up and around my hand. It felt like an electric touch, comforting but still holding me on the edge, anticipating what would come next.

"You feel it?" he asked.

"Yes," I breathed.

"I can call it so easily when I'm with you. When I'm here with you," he told me. "It feels like breathing. Effortless. All because of you, little witch."

The tingling sensation expanded, and I watched with parted lips as the weed began to grow. The shriveled bloom at the tip lifted, coming back to life, and with awe, I saw the petals unfurl, revealing a dark purple so deep it appeared black. The stamens were silver, and the stem blackened beneath our touch.

Beautiful. Not a weed at all.

"A midnight cosmia," I whispered. "But how in the world did it get here?"

Lorik released his grip on my hand. "Their seeds travel far. Keep it in water, and it'll last a lifetime."

"Thank you," I said, bringing it my nose. A beautiful, light fragrance, one that reminded me of quiet summer days, greeted me. "It's a very nice gift."

Lorik jerked, casting a quick look down at his inner wrist.

I frowned. "What's wrong? A glowfly didn't get you, right?"

But I saw no light of one, and Lorik turned his wrist into his side.

"It's nothing," he assured me, smiling. "I'm glad you like the flower."

Hesitantly, I nodded.

Lorik looked around the night garden and then stood from his kneeling position.

"I'll go put it in water," he said, gently taking the bloom from my hand. "And let you finish up out here."

"Yes," I moaned. "Right there—gods, don't stop."

"Mmm," Lorik groaned, capturing my lips as his hips drove into me harder, faster. His pelvis ground down into my clit, and it made me see stars with every thrust. "Going to come for me, little witch? I'm going to join you. Can't hold back any longer."

My nails dug into his back, and Lorik used his wings to propel him forward more forcefully, the gusts sending my curtains fluttering.

"You feel so fucking good," he whispered against my lips, ragged and gruff. "So good, my love."

The orgasm hit me hard, and I cried out, back arching off the bed, my pebbled nipples rubbing against his chest.

"*Yes*," Lorik hissed, his hands on both sides of my head, holding the majority of his weight off me. His hips jerked, his rhythm becoming sporadic, punctuated by sharp thrusts as he followed me in his own release. The heat of his come felt searing—it felt like a brand inside me.

His head was thrown back, the tendons in his neck straining. Behind him his wings gave a gentle gust before sagging. He collapsed on top of me as my pleasure faded, and I gladly took the majority of his weight, though he did keep himself half-held to the side.

He let out a long sigh that rustled my hair, and I felt his lips press to my neck, peppering small, lazy kisses against me. I felt his sweat cooling on my skin and smiled in the afterglow, feeling more relaxed than I had in years. I brought my hand up to his hair, softly combing my fingers through it. He shivered when I scraped at his scalp, giving a little moan into my skin.

When I turned my face to kiss his temple, I savored the warmth and weight of him. Close to my cheek was his wrist from where he'd braced himself. And I—

There was a mark on his wrist that hadn't been there before. Something that shimmered like opals across his skin, something infused with magic, and I suddenly remembered his reaction in the garden. So sudden I'd thought a glowfly had stung him.

It looked like a crest. A shield.

My brow furrowed, and Lorik raised his head. I quickly looked down at him.

"Sorry—I'm crushing you," he murmured lazily. Sleepy already.

"I don't mind it," I told him truthfully. "It feels nice."

What had caused the mark to appear so suddenly? I was certain I would've noticed it before now. I'd been caring for him and his wound, had sat beside him while he'd been sick with infection for nearly an entire day, and he'd been undressed then. No, this mark was new. But what had created it?

And I knew just as certainly that Lorik wouldn't tell me if I asked. There was a part of me that worried he was like Veras—secretive in his business dealings but no less dangerous. What was Lorik involved in? And did I want to know? Or did I just want to enjoy him while I had him? Because even I knew this wouldn't last forever.

Then again, I didn't like to think of myself as a coward.

"Lorik," I said gently, my heart suddenly pounding.

"Hmm?"

"What's that mark on your wrist? I don't think it was there before, right?"

He tensed briefly against my side, though he brought his arm around me, clasping me tightly to him. My bed didn't allow for too much room, but that suited me just fine. His body was stretched behind me, and he tucked my bottom into his groin, his knees drawing up to lock against mine.

"No, it wasn't," he answered. "I'm being summoned."

"Summoned?" I asked, softly incredulous. "Summoned by who?"

"I suppose you could say my employer," he answered wryly. There was a hint of amusement in his tone. "Part of my duty, Marion, is to protect the Black Veil. Against Shades mostly. But when one strays too close to a village, for example, I get summoned to take care of it."

"Then why haven't you gone?" I asked, squirming to turn in his arms so I could face him. "When you say employer—"

"No more questions, you inquisitive thing," he said gently, pressing a kiss to my lips. His eyelids were heavy, but his gaze was soft. "I'm not allowed to answer most anyway."

When he saw the brief flash of frustration cross my features, his expression turned pleading.

"Have patience with me, Marion," he told me. "This is new to me too. A part of me has been alone this long because of this very reason. Because of what I cannot say. There are codes in your Healers' Guild. You are bound to oath, as am I."

When he put it like that…

"All right," I whispered. I nodded against his chest. "I understand."

Lorik blew out a breath. Relief? He kissed my forehead. "Thank you."

"This job of yours…it's not terribly dangerous, is it?"

Lorik chuckled lowly. "Worried for me?"

"A little," I admitted.

"I'm very good at what I do, little witch. You don't have to worry about me."

I...believed it. I'd seen him dispatch the Shade quickly, even injured as he had been. And his injury to begin with...it must've had something to do with this mysterious duty, didn't it?

"I do have to leave, though," Lorik said quietly.

I heard the words. I felt them sink into me and felt icy disappointment spread through my limbs, settling in my belly, making me cold.

"When?" I asked, licking my dry lips.

"Tonight," he answered.

I swallowed, thinking how empty the bed would feel.

"Only for a little while. Then I'll return to you. I promise."

CHAPTER 17

Two nights later, Lorik returned.

I was doing my nightly chores in the garden, bundled in a thick sweater and fur-lined boots since the frost was coming. My mood was dampened, brooding and somber. I thought it was alarming how quickly I could've grown attached to someone, used to their presence in my small, quiet life. I wondered if it was healthy. Logically, I knew I should be wary, but my heart didn't care.

I wanted Lorik. I missed him. His scent, his mischievous grin, his voice. His kisses, his touches, the way he laid me back on my bed and…

I sighed, ignoring the sudden throb between my thighs. My bed smelled like him, which had led to interesting dreams.

More than that, I worried about him. This mysterious job he had…and who he answered to. He was only just recovered from the poisoned arrow. What if something happened to him? What if he never came back?

As if he'd heard that very last thought as I watered the roots of a wrathweed bundle in the bed, I heard his voice, just as I heard Peek's warning hiss.

"Thinking of me, little witch?"

I gasped, whirling, half of the water can spilling outside the bed. But when I saw Lorik standing on the boundary of my property line, just beyond the witch's spell, the can tumbled from my grip and I grinned.

I rushed toward him, and he caught me with a grunt when I accidentally slammed into him a little harder than anticipated.

He felt solid and warm in my arms. I buried my face in his chest, noticing he wore a dark blue vest with subtle silver embroidery and dark pants. In his embrace, I felt a rush of relief so bright that it nearly brought tears springing to my eyes. Then I felt silly, keeping my face pressed to his clothes so he wouldn't see.

"I missed you too, Marion," Lorik murmured, his lips brushing the tip of my ear, his breath hot with the words. He ducked his head, tucking me close.

And I couldn't remember the last time I'd felt so happy.

"We should get out of bed," I whispered to Lorik two mornings later.

"Mmm, no," he replied, keeping my tucked into his body. His front was pressed to my back in my tiny bed, and the heat of him banished the morning chill. "Let's stay here all day. I demand it."

"Demand it?" I asked, smiling, shifting. A small twinge of soreness bloomed between my legs, and there was a fresh bite mark on my neck. Last night—or rather in the early hours of morning—he'd growled that he wouldn't heal it, that he wanted to see his mark on me the next day, that nothing would make him more delighted.

Ever since he'd returned, we'd been ravenous for each other. One would think we'd been separated for months, not mere days.

"I suppose I could be enticed to rise," Lorik murmured, his tone slightly suggestive.

I turned in his arms and propped myself up on my elbow, quirking a brow down at him. "Oh yeah?"

"Yes," he murmured, his eyes strayed down my naked front. My breath hitched when he reached forward to rub a calloused thumb over my pebbled nipple. "What would you entice me with?"

"I know exactly what you want," I said, tone husky from sleep.

Lorik grinned.

"You want those scones I baked yesterday, don't you? Fresh and hot with red riverberry jam spread on top."

"Gods, yes," Lorik groaned. "See? You know me so well already, my love. Let's go."

My laugh was cut off with a brisk kiss, and before I knew it, I was flung up from bed, completely naked. Lorik was up too before I could blink, rummaging through my tiny wardrobe, and I watched as he pulled out a thick sweater and soft green pants.

He had my head through the sweater as the material muffled my giggle.

"Been thinking of those damn scones all night," he grumbled. "You've ruined me, Marion."

He even stooped in front of me to help me put on my pants, sliding his hands up my legs in a thorough way that had me biting my lip. I finished threading my arms through the sleeves of the sweater just as he stood to lace up the pants.

"Now, get in that kitchen, my little witch," he teased against my lips, nipping at the bottom one with his fang. "Or else it's back in bed for you, and I promise you I'll be hungry in other ways that have nothing to do with your scones."

"Hmm, the kitchen or the bed for me? One would think we're back in the Graydom era."

He barked out a sharp laugh. "Believe me, I know how risky

this is to tempt your wrath. I'll make it up to you. But the scones are worth it."

I shook my head, fighting my smile, and went into the kitchen. Behind me, I heard him dressing. One thing I'd learned about Lorik over the last two days was his charmingly voracious appetite for food and the shameless lengths he went to get it. At this rate, we'd have to go to the market to get more provisions because he'd already eaten through half of my underground cellar.

But I didn't mind it. Not one bit. The cottage felt vibrant with him here. It felt brighter, despite the winter approaching.

A Kylorr-Allavari male, I realized, must need to eat a lot.

"Tea?" he murmured, coming up behind me as I stood at my small prep counter. He pressed a kiss to my temple, and my belly erupted in flutters.

"All right," I responded, ducking my head when a huge grin threatened to erupt.

I wasn't used to be taken care of. But Lorik *had* taken care of me the last couple days. In more ways than one. He helped me from the moment we woke until we closed our eyes to sleep. From small things like chores to making my tea in the mornings and evenings to helping in the garden. To larger things like completely fixing two of my back windows and clearing out a clogged pipe from the well.

And then at nights—or really anytime the mood struck—he took care of me in other, more satisfying ways. He was an unselfish lover. Last night, he'd murmured into my ear that it turned him on *more* watching me come apart with his touch.

It felt comfortable between us. Strangely so. Like we'd known each other for years, had lived together for years, had been making love to one another for years...

After Lorik got the kettle on over the hearth, the fire of which he'd stoked with the pile of wood he'd chopped yesterday, he returned to me, leaning against the prep counter, keeping his wings tucked so they didn't get in my way as I mixed the dough.

He watched me. He was dressed in a soft linen tunic, with long sleeves that went to his wrists and dark brown pants, the leather soft and supple with time. He'd cheekily brought a small bag of spare clothes with him on his return. From where? I didn't know. And as the days passed, it got both easier and harder to not ask questions. It was a strange tumultuous feeling bubbling up inside me.

But all I knew was that the inside of his wrist was smooth—no magical marking in sight, calling him away. I'd been checking it the last two nights, even in the middle of the night if I woke and Lorik was sleeping.

"What are you thinking about?" he wanted to know now.

"You," I told him truthfully.

He smiled. He liked that. I could tell.

"I really like you, Marion," he told me softly. I paused in mixing the dough when he reached forward to tuck back a strand of my hair. For a brief moment, I saw his lips pinch down. "One might even say too much."

"Even though we barely know each other?" I asked quietly.

He nodded. He swallowed. Hard.

"Sometimes…I wonder if the Kylorr's deities have been watching over Allavar all this time," he admitted quietly.

I sucked in a sharp breath, feeling my belly warm with the meaning. Fear sprung up too…but only because this felt *real*. This felt meaningful and unlike anything I'd ever experienced before.

He was wondering if fated mates *were* still possible, when he'd told me once he didn't believe in them. He was wondering if I was his. Bound in blood. Picked for one another by a higher power, one that we didn't even understand.

"Oh, Lorik," I breathed.

"Too soon?" he murmured, quirking his lips in a self-deprecating expression. "Maybe. But I don't want to hide what I feel for you, Marion. Because of what? Fear? No, I don't believe in that."

To banish the sudden vulnerability I spied in his eyes, I leaned forward quickly, going up to my tiptoes, and pressed a kiss to his lips. He grunted against me, his hand reaching out to circle my waist. Even though my hands were covered in dough, I cupped his cheek in my grip when I leaned back.

"I really like you too, Lorik," I told him, feeling my throat tighten with fear—but also relief—as I spoke the words. His gaze warmed, molten and soft. "So let's just see where this goes, all right?"

For a long while, Lorik looked like he wanted to say something. I could see the debate in his eyes, the words held on the very tip of his tongue.

But whatever it was died, and I couldn't help but feel a sense of disappointment.

He looked down between us, his eyes going to the floor, and when he met my gaze again, he gave me a warm smile.

"That sounds perfect," he said.

CHAPTER 18

"Fuck, Marion," Lorik hissed, biting the fleshy side of his palm, which squeezed against his mouth. "What else do you need fixed in this place?"

I would've smiled, maybe even laughed at the slight pleading torment in his voice, but my mouth was stuffed, so full that I could only take in a few inches of his cock.

At first, I'd be hesitant. Shy, even. It had been a long time since I'd pleasured a male like this, and my first lover had once told me I wasn't even that good at it. *That* had stung, my self-esteem taking a hit, but Lorik's reaction just about erased years of shame from that one mean, flippant comment.

Or maybe it's just the partner I'm with, I couldn't help but think. Lorik's own obvious pleasure spurred my own. I *wanted* to make him feel better than he ever had before. I *wanted* to make him crazy, I wanted to make him moan and thrash and curse at gods he wasn't sure existed for me.

He'd already made me come. Now it was his turn, and I wanted him to crave this.

I hummed as I slid my lips down his cock, hollowing my cheeks when I reached my limit.

"Gods," he groaned. "Marion, I'm going to come soon. I—"

I released his cock with a wet *pop* and took his length in my hand. Hot and hard, I pumped him, slow and teasing. Silver precome was dripping from his tip at a nearly steady rate, the taste of him lingering on my tongue—earthy and musky and delicious.

"Come for me," I murmured, feeling a distracting throb between my thighs though I ignored it. This was about Lorik. He'd been so generous, and I wanted to return the favor. I'd teased him long enough, however. "I want you to come for me."

His answering groan sounded pained. His hips began to rock against my grip, steady but greedy. I stroked his length, his slippery pre-come and my saliva making my hand glide.

And when I put my lips over the head of his swollen cock, I sucked hard before tracing the seam with my tongue.

His hips punched forward, a hard jerk that I thought took both of us by surprise, but I only tightened my grip on him.

"Fuck, fuck, fuck," he panted, breath huffing out of him. I could see the gleam of his perspiration through his tunic and felt my hands hit the laces of his untied pants every time I ran them down his cock. There was something so very naughty about this. Him fully clothed, on the verge of coming down my throat. And me on my knees before him, not a stitch of clothing on me.

We hadn't even made it the bed. He had his perfect ass wedged against the table, and my knees were pressed to the hard stone floor.

"Marion."

My name was my only warning falling from his lips, and I sucked harder. His hips jerked, a single harsh breath exhaling from his throat, and then he was unleashing his come onto my waiting tongue. The thick ropes of it were hot. Endless. I swallowed him down as best as I could, though some escaped from my lips, dribbling down to my chin.

All the while, Lorik's burning gaze was piercing into me. He *liked* to watch this. I met his eyes as my throat worked, and he whispered something in a language I didn't recognize, though the roots of which sounded Allavari.

When he gave a final jerk against me and I released him, wiping at my face with the dress he'd nearly torn off me, I leaned back on my heels.

For a long while, it was quiet. The crackling in the hearth was the only sound, besides my own heartbeat in my ears.

"You're perfect," he whispered.

"Did you like it?" I couldn't help but ask, suddenly shy, kneeling in front of him, despite what I'd just spent the better of the last twenty minutes doing. My jaw ached from his size, but I needed to hear his praise like I needed air. "If it was bad, you can tell me. I—"

"If it was bad?" Lorik rasped, disbelief in his tone. He straightened, though he didn't bother to tuck himself into his pants before he crouched in front of me. When he kissed me, I gasped. I tried to turn my head away, but he growled, "It turns me on to taste myself on your tongue. You think I'd not like that?"

"Oh," I breathed.

"Why in all the Four Quadrants would you believe it was *bad*?"

"Because…because my first lover told me I was bad at it," I admitted, half wishing I'd not said anything at all.

Lorik's gaze narrowed. "Yeah, well, fuck him. His loss. You're mine now."

My cheeks heated when Lorik threaded his hand behind the nape of my neck, holding me in place when he kissed me again. My heart thudded.

I'm going to fall in love with him, I thought. And for once, the thought didn't bring a stab of fear and trepidation with it.

"And for the record," he murmured against my lips, "I don't remember the last time I came that fucking hard."

"Oh," I whispered, infinitely pleased. "Yeah?"

"Yes," he hissed. "You want to come again?"

"No," I said, biting back my smile in fear it might split open my face.

"You sure?" he purred, pressing teasing kisses to my lips.

I laughed. "Yes."

I pushed at his shoulder, but his hands started to wander.

"All right, let's go bathe, then," he said, helping me up into a standing position. My bones protested, my knees reddened from the hard floor, and Lorik brushed his fingers over them. "I'll get the water hot for you."

"Thank you."

A few moments later, we were situated in the small bathing tub, steam curling around us thanks to Lorik's magic. It was laughable, our position, but someone we'd made it work. Lorik was behind me, his knees drawn up on both sides of me, and I was tucked into his lap. His hands were caressing my body with a soft kind of reverence, and it was lulling me into a trancelike state.

"You're not using magic on me, are you?" I asked sleepily.

"No," he whispered. "Just admiring you."

I grinned lazily, my eyes half-lidded. When had I ever felt this happy, this content with someone? Well, maybe with Aysia, but obviously in a much different way. But with Lorik...I felt comfortable and comforted. I felt *loved*, even though even thinking that word made me a little bashful.

"Thank you for fixing the trellis," I said in the quiet. The washroom was dark. We hadn't bothered to light the candles, but that was all right. Through the small window, there was just enough light from sunset to illuminate the room, casting it in varying shades of lilac and orange. "I can't tell you how long it's been in disrepair."

"I wanted to," he replied, taking the cloth from the edge of the tub, dipping it below the surface. "I want to take care of you, Marion. I want to help you however I can."

"Sometimes I think you're too good to be true," I confessed.

Lorik didn't reply, at least not immediately. He only lathered up the cloth and ran it over the exposed parts of my body before he explored underneath the water.

"I fear one day you'll think quite differently about me."

"Why?" I asked. "Planning to steal all my potions like the last one did?"

He exhaled a sharp breath, but I couldn't tell if it was in amusement or not.

"Where I grew up," he murmured quietly after a brief silence lapsed, "is much different from Rolara. And my father was a very strict male. He had a strong sense of morality, of good and bad. For someone like him, there was no in-between. He couldn't see the differing shades of both, the spectrum of it, even how it can change from one moment to the next. Once you wronged him, you wronged him forever. And he never forgot it, even for his children."

I listened with almost bated breath, fearing that if I made a single move he would get skittish and stop speaking.

"I don't want to be like that," he admitted. "That severe. There is no room for mistakes with someone like that. And all people make mistakes. Even if they think they're right, someone else will think they're wrong."

The back of my neck prickled with something I heard in his voice. Almost like…an apology.

"I imagine that must've been difficult growing up," I said quietly, wishing I could see his face, but he kept me tucked into his front and we both stared at the wall as our words drifted around us. Maybe it was better like this.

"There was very little time to grow up" was what he replied.

"You said you knew you had a purpose. You always knew what you would become," I commented.

"Yes, because of my family's legacy. My father was what I am now. My duty was once his. As was my grandmother's, my grandfather's, and even before them. The line stretches back far. One of us had to take on the duty of it."

"One of us?" I asked quietly.

"My sister. Or my brother at one time," he said. "But it was not what my sister wanted, or even what she was suited for. And my brother...he died long ago."

"I'm sorry," I whispered. "I didn't realize you had lost a sibling as well."

"My father takes on most of the grief these days. He died on a hunt with my father, tracking down a rogue Shade in the north. My brother and I were both trained for the hunts. I just think my father expected it would be Denon to take his position, not me."

I filed away his brother's name in my mind. Denon.

"You want to know the worst part?" he murmured into my ear. "I think my father wishes it was me, not Denon, who had died that day."

"Don't say that," I whispered, not caring that Lorik held me in place for a reason. I struggled to turn in his arms, not caring that there was very little room and that my back ached as I twisted to meet his eyes. "Lorik, don't say that."

"If you ever met my father, you might think differently," he pointed out.

His eyes were glowing *vibrantly*. I could never understand why they did that, if Lorik was simply strumming with magic, if it had to me with me—he'd told me how easily he felt his magic with me—or the cottage—he'd also said that he could feel the magic in the earth of my land.

"I think he hates how good I am at it," Lorik continued, that gaze burning into mine, and I witnessed a side of him I'd never experienced before. His anger. His vulnerability. His hurt. "But I also think he hates himself for it."

"What?"

"I told you...he is only guided by what is right and what is wrong. The code he lives by, the code he's sworn his entire life to.

His morals tell him that he cannot wish death on his other son. What kind of father would he be, then? And he struggles."

"And…and your sister?"

"Thela," he whispered. There was sadness in his tone. "We all would do anything for Thela. She is the good in us all. The best of us all."

There was something I was missing. I could hear it. His tone almost sounded like he was grieving for her.

"Is she…she's not dead, is she?"

Lorik's eyes met mine. Back and forth they flit between them. His brow was furrowed. The sudden change of him was jarring. Even his features seemed sharper, reminding me of that mirage I'd seen when we'd first made love. Gone was the relaxed man who stroked my body gently or whose smile came easy. *This* was Lorik too. The side he hid. Because he didn't want me to see?

But didn't he understand? I wanted to know all of him. I wanted to know every little thing about him, about his upbringing, about his family, about everything that made him smile or what made him angry.

"No," he whispered. "She's not dead."

I pressed my hand to his chest and was surprised when I felt his heart pumping hard beneath it.

"Lorik?" I asked quietly. "What is it? You can tell me—you know that, don't you?"

His eyes closed, and the blue glow from his eyes faded, sinking us further into darkness. I hadn't realized that the sunset's light had gradually begun to fade. Now the washroom was entirely too dark without his eyes.

"She's sick," he murmured.

I straightened. "Sick? With what?"

"An ancient thing," he said, his eyes opening once more. "And no one can help her. Unless…"

"Unless what?" I asked. "Maybe I can help her. Maybe I can—"

He sucked in a sharp breath, his wrist jerking between us. Frowning, my brow furrowed, I watched his gaze go to his inner wrist.

Knowing what it was, I pressed my lips together, already feeling a restlessness take hold.

Whatever it was that Lorik saw, his jaw tightened and he looked at me.

"Maybe I can help her," I said again, feeling desperation claw in my throat. "If I can see her, maybe—"

"I have to go, Marion," Lorik replied.

"What?"

"This summons…it's urgent," he confessed softly. "I have to go."

"*Now?*"

His lips pressed into a hard line, and despite the heat in the bathing tub, I suddenly felt cold. He inclined his head sharply.

"Oh," I whispered. Then I realized I was sitting on him and scrambled to get off. "Of course. I understand."

"I'm sorry," he said. And to his credit, it sounded like it. His jaw was tight, his teeth gritted as he stood from the tub, water sluicing off him.

"Will—will you be back?" I asked.

He must've heard the vulnerability in my tone because he said harshly, earnestly, "*Of course*, Marion. Of course I'll be back. I just need… I don't know how long I'll be gone. But I will be back."

In my mind, I thought, *And how much longer will we be able to keep each other when he is always pulled somewhere else?*

Lorik leaned down to press a hard kiss to my lips.

"Wait for me?" he asked against my lips. "Then we can continue this conversation, I promise."

How long? I wondered.

"All right," I whispered, looking up at him when he pulled away. "Be careful."

"I always am, little witch."

Then he was gone. I heard him dress, I heard the front door to my cottage close. And I was alone again, sitting in the tub that was still hot with his magic.

I was alone again…only this time it felt so much worse.

CHAPTER 19

Market day in Rolara had always been something I'd dreaded. A necessity, though I'd always felt the lingerings of guilt when villagers lined up near my usual stall before I even arrived.

I should enjoy this more, I'd always thought as I'd lugged my cart of potions all the way from the Black Veil into the village. Every month, like clockwork. People depended on my potions. They made their lives better. And it *did* make me content. There was a sense of pride in my work.

But I was no longer the fresh-faced, starry-eyed recruit in the Healers' Guild as I once had been. I'd hidden myself away after Aysia's tragic death, unable to take the whispers and pitying looks that followed me everywhere I went. I was comfortable in the Black Veil, comfortable in my solitude with my glowflies and Peek for company.

Every month, as I lugged my cart to the market, there was a sense of duty now. Duty because I was a keeper of glowflies and the keeper of the rarest of them all—shadevines. Duty because I'd taken an oath, bound in magic. Duty because…well, I needed the money to keep my cottage running, to buy any provisions I needed, and to pay the witch for the monthly protection spell.

So, no, I didn't enjoy going to the market under normal circumstances.

But today?

Today, I hurried from the Black Veil at the crack of dawn and made for Rolara.

When I'd first encountered Lorik all those months ago, when he'd sauntered up to my stall with a mischievous smirk, his keen eyes scanning my table, covered in a cloth with holes in it…that day had begun to make market days a little more interesting. Because I always knew *he'd* be there. I'd had a silly, childish, fun crush on the mysterious Kylorr-Allavari male…

Only now I knew him. I knew he was as charming as he looked. I knew he could kiss me until I felt like I was floating and that he made my tea perfectly in the mornings. I knew the way his arms felt around me, how they made me feel safe and protected.

I knew I liked him and he liked me too. And I knew that I was in danger of falling in love with him. And I knew he'd left me in the washing tub nearly four days ago and he hadn't come back…

My heart was in turmoil, a maelstrom of emotions. Elation and hope that I could see him today—because he'd *always* been at the market days. Disappointment and hurt because I felt abandoned, with no indication of when I'd see him next.

When I reached the town's outskirts, I saw that the banners and streamers signaling the market day had been put up overnight. Colorful ribbons that danced in the cold breeze. Most of the vendors during the event had their own shops in the village…but there was a sense of community and excitement surrounding the market, a small celebration in itself to close out the end of every month. There would be music and dancing and food. And overpriced items that you could buy for half the following day in the village.

I wasn't the only one to arrive early, and I nodded at the familiar faces as I passed. I'd arrived so early today that there wasn't a line for once in my usual place, and I felt a sense of relief. I could take my time this morning, arrange things *just so*.

And most importantly, I could keep an eye out for Lorik.

But the morning came and went. Lorik didn't show. He was nowhere to be seen. And in between fulfilling orders and stashing away coins in my pouch, chatting with customers who always asked probing questions about the Black Veil and how I could stand to live in such a desolate empty place, and dodging any sympathetic comments about my sister—which I still received even now…I never saw him once.

As the morning stretched into the afternoon, I started to get worried. He'd never missed a market day, and he'd said his summoning was urgent. What if something had gone wrong? What if…what if he was injured?

I sold the last of my potions long before the market was over. And still, I sat at my stall. I ventured over a food stand selling smoked-meat sandwiches with root chips, and it tasted like ash in my mouth. I wandered the market, my purse of coins clinking noisily against my hip, though I tried to keep it muffled so a brazen thief didn't get any ideas.

But as vendors began to pack up their carts, I felt a slump of defeat, worry, and disappointment. And I began to do the same.

I finished quickly, now eager to leave because the dark could come soon and I didn't want to trek through the Black Veil at night. But I could hear the crunch of footsteps behind me as someone approached.

"I'm all out of everything," I told them when they cleared their throat. I had my back turned, had been used to saying the words all afternoon. "I'm sorry."

"Never thought I'd hear those words coming from your lips, Marion," came a familiar voice.

My teeth grit, a surge of distaste going through me, even though I'd decided to try to move on.

Remember what you decided, I told myself.

When I turned, I saw Veras there. His guard stood a handful of paces away, giving us the illusion of privacy.

"Veras," I greeted as politely as I could manage. Just because I'd decided to move on…it didn't mean I had to like him. I likely never would.

His smile was small, his eyes assessing as he studied me and my cleared table. I imagine other females would find him very attractive—Aysia certainly had—but I just felt nauseous thinking about him in that way.

"Good day at the market?" he asked.

"It always is," I said back, raising a brow. When his lips quirked, I blew out a small breath, casting a look to the sky, at the sinking sun. "Habit. Seeing your face just brings out the bitch in me."

Veras barked out a sharp laugh. "I'm one of the only Allavari who wouldn't take offense to *you* telling me to fuck off, Marion. For others? Not so much."

"Why are you here?" I asked, ignoring what went unspoken —that he treated me differently than he treated others. Because of Aysia. "Market days aren't usually your priority as you make your rounds."

"I told you before—I've always watched out for you, Marion."

"But you never needed to show your face to do it," I said back, tossing the hole-ridden tablecloth into my empty cart. I needed to speak to the witch before I left, to schedule her to come to the Black Veil soon, and I was suddenly impatient to leave.

"I'll walk you back," he said after a lengthy silence. He wasn't dressed in his usual clothes. He looked almost…casual. Gray pants and a black coat, though both were still expertly tailored with a talented hand. His boots even had a scuff on them. "It's getting dark."

"I don't need your help."

"I'm not asking," he murmured, his eyes straying behind me to the line of trees in the distance. "The Black Veil has seen more and more Severs coming through."

I jerked my head up to him. "What do you mean?"

"Just that the activity is increasing," he told me, his gaze returning to mine. "My guard and I will escort you back to your property line. We won't step foot inside. Then I'll leave. You don't even have to speak to me on the journey, but there is something I want to say to you."

I knew it, I thought, both worried about what he'd tell me for Lorik's sake and annoyed because he likely wanted something from me. An antidote for one of his men, perhaps? He'd asked before.

"I don't have any more night nettle for antidotes," I informed him.

"It's not that," he said, smiling.

"I still have to talk to the witch."

He shook his head. "I'll pass on your request to her tonight. I'll be in that direction anyway for a dinner party."

I hesitated for only a moment more. The sky *was* darkening quite rapidly over our heads—and it looked like a storm might've even been brewing—and I didn't want any trouble home.

"Fine," I told him. "You can escort me home. But don't think I'll serve you tea afterward. You leave when we get there."

"Can I visit her grave at least?" he wondered.

I exhaled a sharp breath, a soft note in his voice making me feel guilty.

"Yes."

"Did you…did you give her the wreath?" he asked next.

"Yes," I said, sighing. "I did."

"Thank you," he murmured. I nodded and went to take the handles of my cart. "Emell will get the cart—don't worry about it."

His guard, I realized when the hulking Kylorr stepped forward, inclining his head at me. I let it be—there was nothing worth stealing in it anyway—and walked toward the boundary of the Black Veil.

Vendors packing up their wares observed us as we passed, but I kept my head down to avoid their stares. Veras, however, smiled and greeted everyone we passed. Ever charming, keeping up appearances. I nearly snorted.

When we entered the line of the forest, Rolara faded away and there was a sense of relief that wiggled through my bones. Veras, however, seemed on edge. He didn't like the Black Veil. Which was ironic because I'd always thought he, out of anyone, should feel the most at home in its dark, rotting depths.

But instead…it was me.

Behind us, I heard Emell pull the cart over a fallen log, but Veras got right to it.

"Where's your lover?" he asked. "Lorik, isn't it?"

Veras knew perfectly well what his name was.

"You wanted to talk to me about Lorik?" I clarified, casting him an observing look. He slid his arm through a canopy of low-hanging vines from the tree above, like he was parting a curtain for me, and I stepped through it.

"Yes," he said. "I wanted to warn you about him."

I stilled on the unmarked path, though I knew the way to my cottage like the back of my hand. Turning to face him, I leveled him a look with narrowed eyes. I was torn. One part of me wanted to defend Lorik, to tell Veras to stay out of my business. The other part? He knew something about Lorik that I didn't. Something I wanted to know…but it would betray Lorik's trust if I asked, wouldn't it?

But he'd been gone for four days. I hadn't heard a single thing, not a delivered note or a scrap of a message. I didn't even know when I'd see him again because he'd given me *nothing*.

"I don't know where he is," I said, answering his question. There was no harm in answering a question wasn't it? "He didn't tell me."

"Ah," Veras murmured.

I started walking again, but I didn't hear the creak of my cart nor Veras's footsteps as he followed.

"Lorik is a Sever, Marion."

CHAPTER 20

I froze.

Ice pierced my blood at the words, my belly churning with disbelief. And yet…

I'd thought it myself once, hadn't I? The possibility?

Veras stepped up beside me, and I felt his warm hand on my arm.

"How…how do you know that?"

My sister's once-in-a-lifetime love exhaled a sharp breath though his nostrils before his eyes scanned the dark forest in front of us.

"Tell me," I demanded.

"Do you know where the portal to the Below is?" Veras asked.

"No," I said, still reeling from his confession. I didn't want to believe it…and yet it still rang true in my ears. "Of course not."

"I do," Veras told me. "And I've seen Lorik Ravael coming and going often over the years. I had him tracked once. One of the best trackers in all of Allavar—Lorik never even knew he was there."

"Why did you have him tracked?"

"A stranger turns up in Rolara. No one knows him. No one

knows where he came from. There's an air about him that told me he was different. Dangerous. Despite what you think, I do what I can to protect Rolara from outsiders."

"Oh, really? Like the Jetutians you brought on planet?"

"Marion," Veras said, gritting his teeth, a brief flash of anger flitting over his face, though he kept it controlled.

I glared.

"I had him followed," Veras said, ignoring my barb, "years ago. I saw him entering the portal. It suddenly made sense. Severs have been among us for years. Much more often than the ignorantly blissful villagers back there would like to think."

"What?" I whispered, my lips parting. "But…wouldn't they be noticed?"

"Did it ever cross your mind that Lorik could be a Sever?" Veras asked, cocking his head to the side. I pressed my lips together. "How about…your old shopkeeper friend? Merec? That was his name, wasn't it?"

"Merec," I repeated, dumbstruck.

Lorik had said…gods, he'd said that Merec had been friends with his father, that his debt had been to a Sever. He'd told me the truth of it, hadn't he? Only I hadn't really *understood* what he'd been telling me.

"Severs have been living among us for over two hundred years, and very few even know," Veras told me, his tone almost… gentle. "*That* is what power buys you, Marion. *Knowledge.* And it's a priceless thing. A veil lifted from your own eyes."

I stumbled forward a few steps, dragging in a deep breath. The sunlight from above the canopies was fading fast. Darkness was falling in the Black Veil, but I was rooted into place like the trees around me.

"And I think you deserve to have it lifted from yours," Veras told me. "So you can see him for what he clearly is."

"Even…even if he is a Sever…he's not a Shade."

"Ah, so he has told you something," he murmured. "He

might not be a Shade, Marion, but he's even more dangerous. Severs…"

He trailed off, and I looked back at him curiously when I heard his hesitation.

"It's in their best interest to make us all believe Shades are Severs. Monsters in the dark to help protect their world, their precious portal. Stories that have been circulating for years to frighten children and keep villagers on their toes. To keep them away from the Black Veil."

"There are dangers here," I said quietly. "I've seen them."

"I never said there weren't," Veras replied. "But Severs protect their world because it's *better*. Their magic runs freely, an untapped well of magic in the Below."

My lips parted, understanding dawning. Lorik was powerful indeed. Was that why?

"And they don't want the Above dwellers to know. As our magic fades from the land, as our crops fail and our talents begin to wither."

"That's not true," I whispered, though my voice held no true conviction. "They aren't taking it from us. We've just…forgotten how to channel it."

Veras smiled. "Is that what your lover told you? And tell me, Marion, what's in his best interest?"

I went quiet, my heart pounding in my chest with this influx of new information. Things I didn't want to believe because that meant that Lorik had lied about a lot more than I even imagined to believe.

"How do you know all this?" I asked.

"Power, like I told you," Veras told me. "Lorik is dangerous, Marion. He's the right hand of the Below King—a powerful position. A hunter. A mercenary. And they're up to something, something even my spies cannot discern because it is kept close to the royal court. Don't let him keep you in the dark. In fact, it's better if you stay away from him entirely."

Veras came to stand in front of me. He tilted my chin up so that I met his eyes. I was reeling, so shocked that I didn't even react to his touch. I was frozen in place, and I felt...betrayed. I felt like a fool.

"I never had a sister," he said quietly. "I told you before—we are bound by our love for *her*, Marion. For Aysia. Forever. And so you are the closest thing to a sister I will ever have."

I swallowed hard, overwhelmed by everything. This was too much. It was *too much*.

"I know you don't want me to look after you, but I promised Aysia that I would."

"You...you did?" I whispered.

He nodded, his expression solemn. "So take my words to heart. This is not a path you want to travel. They are infinitely more powerful than us...and they have a lot more to lose. He hasn't told you anything else, has he?"

I jerked my chin back and took a step away. "I'm not one of your spies, Veras," I said, keeping my voice even, letting him know I knew what he was doing. "But no, he hasn't."

His sister, I thought. Or had that been a lie?

Either way, I wouldn't tell Veras that. Some habits died hard, despite his pretty words about Aysia. I still didn't trust him. And after this conversation, I certainly didn't trust Lorik.

"You're...you're absolutely certain of Lorik?" I asked. I couldn't help it. "I mean *absolutely* certain?"

Veras tilted his chin back. "On Aysia, I swear it."

So, it was the truth. Or at least a truth that Veras believed, and I knew that Veras wasn't a blundering fool. He was smart, cunning.

I said nothing else. There was nothing else *to* say.

Instead, I turned in the direction of my cottage as thoughts raced through my mind. And I kept on walking...because I wasn't sure what else I could do.

CHAPTER 21

The next night, it was Peek's sudden, warbling hiss that had me standing from my chair. His back was arched, fur standing on end, ears pricked forward.

It had been storming all day, a torrential downpour of icy rain that stung my skin, but right then it was a light pattering on my roof. For a moment I thought there might be a Shade outside. Peek never reacted like that unless there was danger near.

But when I went to my window and glimpsed out, my heart stopped in my chest.

Lorik.

Standing on the edge of my property, his clothing soaked, hair plastered to his skull.

He saw me looking through the window, but he didn't make a step toward the cottage. Taking a deep breath, I grabbed my heaviest shawl from the peg near the door and stuffed my feet into my boots.

I'd been in a daze since my talk with Veras yesterday evening. I'd run through nearly every interaction I'd ever had with Lorik, starting from the beginning, analyzing every conversation we'd had. What he'd said about the Below, about Severs, about Shades, about Allavari.

And what I'd come to realize was that I didn't know anything at all.

Veras had been right. It *was* like a veil being pulled back from your eyes. How could you ever go back?

Before I stepped foot outside, my gaze caught on my chest near the door. I hesitated a mere moment…but then I grabbed a small dagger and hid it in the pleats of the shawl.

The chill outside was bone-numbing, but I trudged toward Lorik, my mouth set in a thin line. I didn't know what I would say to him. I'd tried to plan it all out, but the words stuck in my brain. Like a funnel, they all got clogged up toward the end.

Lorik hadn't taken a step forward. For a moment, I wondered about that. He was inside the barrier spell, but he hadn't taken a step toward the cottage.

When I could make out his face in the dark, I saw that he looked tired. There was a hardness in his features—one that softened briefly when he first saw me—that hadn't been there before. He seemed in no hurry to get inside from the rain, not that I would let him. I needed answers. I needed them tonight.

No more hiding. No more fear.

I stopped when we were a few arms' lengths apart. The hilt of my small dagger felt hot in my palm despite the cold.

Lorik studied me. The longer he studied me, the more realization settled into the lines of his features, deepening his frown, the space between his brow growing darker when he furrowed it.

"Marion."

I felt something crack in me at my name.

"Why can't you take a step toward me?" I asked.

His jaw ticked. He looked down at the ground between us, and I wondered what he saw.

"Is it because what you said is true? That Peek really does protect me from Severs?"

Lorik's head rose slowly, his eyes beginning to glow blue.

Finally, he said, "Your *braydus* drew its own barrier here. You've changed your mind about me. Peek senses it and will not let me cross."

How could I have been such a fool?

"So many things that I willfully ignored," I said quietly. "Why? Because I was lonely? Because I was that desperate for affection and intimacy and touch?"

"Marion…" Lorik rasped, running a hand through his slick hair, combing it back away from his face. Rain shimmered across his cheekbones as moonlight filtered into the clearing.

And I didn't know who he was at all.

Then he sighed, a rough exhale. I watched the light shift off his face. That familiar shimmering I'd only caught glimpses of, writing them off as a trick of the light. Then, with parted lips, I watched as his features changed, his body growing slightly larger, slightly taller.

Another veil dropping from my eyes.

Him.

It was that image I'd caught when we'd first made love. His features were sharper, more beautiful, more cutting. The tips of his ears were like knives, and his ethereal blue eyes glowed even brighter. His jawline widened. His skin silvered even more, practically glowing in its luminosity.

"Magicked glamour," he explained, though his voice didn't change. "Difficult to hold, and it takes energy. It's why the infection took root…because I was using most of my strength to sustain the glamour, even in my sleep."

"Who even are you?" I whispered. I feared my words would be carried away by the sudden gusting of wind, bringing in another dark cloud bank from the west.

"I'm the same as I was, Marion," Lorik said, attempting to step forward, to reach forward…but he hit something. Peek's magic. Peek's barrier. He'd been telling the truth about one thing at the very least…and I'd never even known. "I swear that to you."

"No, I never knew you," I said, my shoulders dropping. "Lies upon lies. And maybe you didn't outright lie to my face, Lorik. But you certainly weaved. And avoided. Anything not to tell me the truth."

"I am bound by *oath*, Marion," he insisted, a pleading note entering his tone. His face was the same, but the structure was all different. More rugged, more roughly handsome than the delicate Allavari features I'd come to know. "I cannot say things without punishment."

I certainly understood that. But there were ways around it… and he'd never even *tried* to help me understand.

"Tell me the truth now."

His sharp jaw tightened. There was a scar just underneath his chin, a scar that hadn't been there before, one he'd hidden with this glamour. I remembered what Veras had told me, that Severs had been living among us for a lot longer than anyone realized… and perhaps this was how.

Because no one would look at Lorik in his true form and *not* know there was something otherworldly about him.

He was Allavari and he was Kylorr…but he was much, much more. His bloodline must've run back generations.

"Marion," he said quietly.

"The truth. Or I walk back into my cottage and we will never speak again. Whatever oath you took be damned—I deserve to know the truth, Lorik."

I wondered what his punishment would be. I wondered what the magic would take of him. I understood blood oaths. I'd taken one myself. If I didn't help someone when I knew they were in need…I would feel their pain acutely.

Maybe that was part of why I'd hidden myself away in the Black Veil. Because it was easier to ignore others' suffering. Because it was no great risk to me. I hated the cowardly part of myself. But Lorik had been the last person I'd helped…and look where that had gotten me.

With the oath in mind, I didn't expect the truth from him. Not truly.

And so I began to turn away. It would feel like an unfinished chapter in my life, but I would accept that to spare my heart. I'd always told myself to never fall in love. Love only brought pain. Suffering. In Aysia's case, death.

Fool, I thought, fighting back tears, feeling that empty loneliness creeping back inside me as I remembered how content I'd felt lying next to Lorik in my small bed. Of hearing his breathing and feeling his heart against my back. Of memorizing the veins in his wings and the way his eyes gleamed when he was looking at me.

They were things I didn't need to remember because it would make the loss of him hurt all the more.

"I'm a Sever, Marion."

I froze, not looking at him but not quite leaving either.

"Though we call ourselves Kelvarians, not Severs. That's an old word, a distasteful one to us."

The rain began to pick up, icy pinpricks on my flesh, sliding down my cheeks like tears.

"I was born in the Below. It is my home. It is where I live. It is what I know," Lorik went on. His voice almost took on a trancelike property, and I found myself looking over my shoulder at him, studying the conflict over his changed features. "I am the Below King's Hunter. A high position in his court, and I do whatever he tasks me with, for the safety and security of our home. My father was the Hunter before me, his father before him. It was my purpose after my brother died. That is what I am."

I turned to face him but didn't take a step forward to close some of the gap between us.

"For such a high-ranking position in his court, why bother

coming to the Above world at all?"

Lorik exhaled sharply. "Shades come from our world. They are a product of us, of a darker time and history in the Below. It didn't seem right to let them run freely in your world, when we knew their potential and their crimes."

"Then why come to the villages?" I asked. "Shades stay in the Black Veil, don't they?"

"For the most part, yes," Lorik replied, studying me carefully. "I wanted to know the villages better. I'd heard stories of the Above for most of my life—tales from my mother. I was curious. And I found they weren't as terrible as they'd always been described to us."

I released a shaky breath.

"And then…I saw a human woman at a market day in Rolara," he continued, his voice softening. "With beautiful hair, the color of which I'd never seen before, and soft, almost sad eyes…and I wanted to know more about her."

"Don't," I whispered, shaking my head.

"That's why I came to Rolara, Marion," he said…but I didn't know if I could believe him. I wanted to, but I didn't know what to believe anymore.

"And the arrow?" I asked, hardening my voice. "The poisoned arrow?"

His features shuttered, a brief flash of shame appearing until he smoothed it from his expression with furrowed brow, lines appearing between them.

"I need something from you," he told me quietly.

"What?" I asked, surprised. Then I laughed. "What could you possibly…"

Realization hit.

"Oh," I said. A flash of bitterness rose in me. I laughed, but it sounded like a choke. "You're no better than the rest of them, are you?"

Lorik's expression was pained. Again, he tried to step forward before he remembered himself. "It's not like that—I need you to believe me. Just let me explain."

"Then explain," I said. "And don't you dare lie."

"The arrow…the injury…the poisoning…it was all planned," Lorik said, the words released in a rush, like a purging. "From the very beginning."

I stared at him, hardly registering his words. My heart thudded in my ears until I could barely hear anything else.

"But *please*, Marion, know that I never acted the way I did…I never pretended when I was with you," Lorik said quickly, his words a dizzying rush.

"All you did was pretend," I said, my tone hollow. "Were you truthful about anything?"

"About the way I feel about you, yes!" he urged. "But you have to understand this is bigger than me. The entire Below is threatened, Marion. This wasn't about what I wanted. This was my duty, to help my people, my *family*."

I looked away from him, to glance into the Black Veil. I wondered how far the portal was from my cottage. Was it near where I'd found him, leaning against a tree, an arrow in his shoulder?

"The arrow was planned. I ordered one of my huntsman to strike me with it," he confessed. "I knew your healer's oath. I took advantage of that. Even the poison was taken into account…I knew you would send me on my way if it was a mere flesh wound. I needed to…"

"You needed to get close to me so that I would do what you wanted," I finished for him, the ugly truth tumbling from my lips. "You manipulated me. You tricked me. You used me. You made me like you so that in the end, I would do what you wanted."

Lorik's eyes closed briefly, his features scrunching up, his breaths coming fast.

"The shadevine queen, right?" I guessed. "That's what you want. That's what they always want."

Lorik met my eyes, that glow illuminating the sprinkling of rain between us.

"Not the queen," he murmured. "I need the hive heart."

I choked out a laugh of disbelief, and it sounded like a sob.

"The heart. Without it, the queen will abandon the hive. All her glowflies will die without the heat. All the shadevines will wither in the garden," I told him, numbness beginning to take root.

"I know," he murmured quietly. "But many will die without it."

"Why not just steal it?"

"The heart needs to be freely given," he rasped.

"Why?" I asked, my tone chipped like ice.

"Our most powerful Kelvarian sorceress demands it for her spell," Lorik told me, his shoulders sagging slightly, his wings dipping into the wet, mushy soil beneath him. "The hive heart must be freely given."

"So that's why you needed the deception. That's why you pretended to—"

"I never pretended, Marion," Lorik snapped. "I was disappointed that it had to be you."

I flinched.

"Not in that way. Fuck!" Lorik cursed, bringing a hand up to his horn. "I was agonizing over what needed to be done. For *weeks*. But you are the only one—the *only one*—who possesses a shadevine hive. No other healers' guild, no glowfly keeper within two week's flying distance has one. Because, believe me, I searched. It was a miracle that you have one. It *had* to be you. And I never wanted to hurt you. I never wanted to betray you, Marion, but this was the only choice. The only way to save my people."

I turned from him.

"Marion!"

He thought I was leaving, but I only paced a short distance away before I rounded back.

"What's the spell for?" I demanded. "You said people would die?"

Lorik opened his mouth, words perched on the edge on his tongue. Was this what he couldn't tell me? What his oath was bound to? Or had he already broken it?

"Kelvarians created Shades. Long ago," he told me, his tone grave. "I told you we have a dark history with Shades. It…it wasn't right. It was a terrible thing, a sordid past that not many speak about today. But something is happening in the Below, little witch."

I bit my cheek at the pet name he'd given me. Once meant to tease, it felt like a caress. Only now? It was one I didn't want.

"Someone powerful is creating Shades again with the same dark magic that opened the portal to the Below over two hundred years ago. It's a sickness, a plague that's spreading through our city and the surrounding villages. My sister…"

My breath squeezed from my lungs. His sister? He'd said she was sick. It had been with *this*?

Or it's another lie, I couldn't help but think, bitterness and anger eating me up.

"My sister started showing the signs of it nearly a month ago. She took a turn for the worse. That's why I had to leave, Marion. Why I was called back so urgently. Why I've been gone. This dark magic…it's almost consumed her. And once it does, there's no way to go back. There's no cure for this. Only death would be a relief. She would spend the rest of her days like a ghost. She wouldn't be able to speak, food would taste like ash in her mouth, she would no longer feel the warmth of moonlight, and love would wither away in her chest."

What he spoke of…could something horrible like that exact?

But then I remembered the Shade we'd encountered, very

near to where Lorik was now. Lorik had told me the Shade had *wanted* to die. He'd said it was a mercy.

"I cannot see my sister go through that," Lorik confessed. "I would do anything to help her. To help all the Kelvarians who are afflicted with this cruel spell. Even if it means you hate me for it, Marion. Because this is bigger than *us*, even if I wish, out of all the people in this world, that you weren't the one who has exactly what I need."

I didn't know why I believed him.

But I did. I believed that he was telling me the truth about whatever was happening in the Below. Maybe that made me the biggest fool in the entire universe. Maybe that was why I didn't trust anyone…because maybe I trusted too easily at first and never learned my lesson.

I heard the sad truth in Lorik's voice. I saw it in his glowing eyes and in the pinching frown on his face, his features strange yet familiar to me.

I'd had the shadevine hive for years, had tended to it for years. The loss of it would feel like a dagger to my own chest… but how could I be that selfish?

"Wait here," I said, my voice hollow. "Not that Peek would let you cross."

Then I did what I knew was right, even if it hurt. With ice in my heart, I approached the night garden, walking beneath the trellised entrance with slow steps. Only some of the glowflies were out in this storm—the majority of them were hunkered in their warm hives.

I approached the shadevine hive, trying to keep my tears from spilling down my cheeks. I hated what I had to do, but I'd always known…I would always sacrifice my glowflies for Allavari lives. Or apparently Kelvarian lives too.

Without a second thought, my cold hand shot into the hive, securing my fist around the warm heart—spongy in texture, the home of the queen—which seemed to beat under my palm with its magic. I could feel the glowflies wiggling against my hand, confused and agitated.

"I'm sorry," I whispered. Then I plucked out the heart. The queen was inside, and I watched her crawl out as the storm picked up. She stung me on the back of my hand, the prick worse than a dagger—making me hiss in pain and bite my lip to keep from crying out—and then she disappeared…flying off into the night.

Gone. Just like that.

The rest of the glowflies buzzed around me, a halo of blue light like Lorik's eyes. None of them stung me, however—only their queen had. I watched as they flew in dizzying circles, desperate in their confusion.

Lorik was watching me with sad eyes when I returned to him. The heart in my hand felt spongy. It felt soft and warm—a living, magical thing that I had stolen. Was this freely given when *I* had taken it?

"Here," I said, keeping my voice even, despite the tears that rolled down my face. Grief built in my chest. For my glowflies, for Lorik's betrayal, and for the strange sense of loss and heartbreak I felt.

Peek's barrier kept him from reaching forward, so I stretched out the hive heart to him. He took it, his fingertips brushing mine. I snatched my hand back when he made to reach for it.

"Take it," I told him.

"Marion—"

"But I never want to see you again," I said, cutting him off. "Good luck."

And goodbye, I thought silently.

Then I turned…and I didn't look back.

CHAPTER 22

"Take two drops in some tea every evening, all right?" I told the elderly Allavari woman. I stoppered the vial, making sure the seal was tight. "It'll help with your mobility."

"Does it matter which tea?" she wondered, a concerned look on her face as I helped her stand from the bench. The soothing light of the guild hall's front room was golden, meant to replicate fire light. It *was* calming, but I remembered Eymaris as always being a worrier. She hadn't changed in nearly ten years. "Because I cannot stomach that tea blend the shops stock. Tastes like flowers! Who wants to drink flowers?"

I bit back my sigh and gave her a soft smile instead, ushering her to the door since I needed to get back to my cottage.

"Any tea will do," I assured her, opening the door, watching her clutch the black bottle of concentrated lovery leaf oil and night nettle, my own special blend, like her life depended on it. "Try the skyberry one. They have it at Griffel's shop."

"Griffel's," Eymaris repeated, as if she needed to speak it to remember it. She gave a long sigh. "I'll go now and see if they have any. I simply cannot stand that flower tea."

I bit back my smile. "Hurry, then, before they close. Remember—just two drops in the tea."

"Two drops," she repeated.

I watched her walk down the cobbled pathway, my lungs squeezing a little when she stumbled over a dislodged rock before she managed to catch herself. She went on her way, and I set out to the path, stamping down the rock and covering it with a heavy layer of soil to keep the edges close to the ground.

When I looked up at the sky, I saw night was approaching and fast. And so I went back inside the Healers' Guild hall, made sure everything was in order in the front room before I left. The next healer scheduled would arrive in mere moments, and I had no more patients for the evening.

As I walked through Rolara at dusk, I admired the brightly lit shop windows, calmed by the thud of my boots on the paved roads, and took in the chatter from passing families and the laughter pouring through windows.

It had been my favorite time of day in the last two weeks, ever since I'd given Lorik the hive heart. The time where the world quieted, people returned to their families, shops closed their doors, and warm light illuminated the darkening streets.

"Good evening, Marion," called a familiar voice. Gwilor, an older Kylorr male who I had treated at the guild hall the week prior.

"Evening," I greeted back as we passed, giving him a small smile.

Another called out to me toward the end of the street. Winnand, an Allavari-Ernitian female, with thick, long blue hair and yellow eyes. She was a baker of Ernitian delicacies and had sliced her hand open on a sharp knife a few days ago.

"How's it healing?" I asked as we passed.

She held up her palm, flashing me a smile. It hadn't quite deep been enough to require stitching, but I was pleased with the progress.

"Almost back to normal!" she reported. "I'll drop off some pastries at the guild hall for you tomorrow. The ones I told you about."

"I'm looking forward to it," I told her. I smiled and waved her off, my strides a little more upbeat. Even as I passed Grimstone's Tavern tonight, laughter and conversation filtering from the windows, it didn't dampen my mood.

My footsteps hushed as I stepped on the dirt-lined path of Market Row, where I sold my goods every month, and then the Black Veil loomed before me. For once, it didn't seem like a relief to enter its shadowed depths. For once, I wondered if I should go back to Grimstone's, order a goblet of wine after the day, sit in a back booth, and *not* think of Lorik.

When I'd made the decision to return to the Healers' Guild, to take on a shift every single day, I hadn't quite known what to expect. Only that I'd *needed* to. I'd felt that need so strongly in my chest that it had felt crushing.

It was partly to do with Lorik. My aching heart hadn't been able to withstand the quiet of my cottage and the familiarity of the daily routine I'd created there. I'd been restless, grieving, overthinking, heartbroken, and angry…and I knew if I didn't change *something*, it would drive me mad.

Lorik had been the catalyst…but I'd known for a long time, hadn't I? I'd known that if I didn't start living a different life, if I didn't start filling it with things I wanted, not things that were comfortable and familiar, then I would die alone. I would never know love. I would never have a family of my own. I would become bitter and angry. And I didn't want to be.

The night after I'd given Lorik the shadevine-hive heart, I'd had a dream that I'd transformed into a Shade. A lifeless, soulless Shade, wandering the Black Veil, in search of something but never quite being able to find it.

I'd woken in a cold sweat, crying, gripping my chest as if I could've squeezed my hand around my heart like I had in the hive.

That morning, I'd gotten dressed…and I'd gone straight into Rolara. Nothing had deterred me from my path to the Healers' Guild hall, tucked against the north end of the village, and I'd gone straight to Salladar, the head of the guild. I'd told him I wanted a daily shift, one he'd hesitantly given me. It'd had nothing to do with my ability. Salladar knew my ability better than anyone…he'd trained me himself, after all, when I'd first started my studies after leaving Correl's.

But the sudden change in me had likely startled him, whereas all I'd felt was determination and desperation. I'd taken an oath to help the people of Allavar. I'd turned my back on it in the last decade. I could understand his reluctance. I didn't know what he'd seen in my eyes that morning, but he'd let me stay, on the condition that I helped with the guild's glowflies once every week.

The pay was meager, but it gave me a renewed sense of purpose again. I talked to more people in a day than I had in the previous month combined. People began to greet me in town, the whispers beginning to die out though I did still catch a few now and again—no doubt curious why I was in Rolara every day. I'd even caught sight of Veras a few times, but he'd only nodded at me, his familiar guard always trailing him. There was an unspoken truce between us. Tentative but there.

And in the evenings, I returned to my cottage. If Peek was displeased that I was away from the cottage for longer some days, he didn't show it. My only worry in returning to the cottage every night was that I'd be gone too long.

After I'd taken the shadevine-hive heart, I'd done my absolute best to keep the remaining glowflies alive without the queen. I heated a large spherical river rock every morning and every evening. I woke in the middle of the night at least once too. It was large enough that it kept the entire hive warm for hours, and

I figured it must've been working because the glowflies were still alive. Even without the queen, they still worked for me, tending to the shadevines.

I didn't know how long it would work. But I would wake up every hour in the dead of winter if it meant saving them. I owed it to them.

Walking through the Black Veil now, I wondered what I would do in a few weeks when the sun would set long before my shift at the guild hall ended.

Veras had said that more and more Shades were roaming the Black Veil, and while I had yet to encounter one on my walks home, I knew it might only be a matter of time. I'd always seen them, here and there. They stayed far away, and I knew that Peek would protect me. But knowing that there was unrest in the Below, that Lorik was frightened about something…it had made me uneasy every single night.

I never breathed a sigh of relief until I stepped beyond Peek's boundary, and I wondered if I should start bringing him into Rolara with me for extra protection come winter.

Peek might even like it, I thought. He could wander the streets and spy on people while I worked in the guild hall.

A branch snapped in the Black Veil, and I froze on the path, my heart pounding in my chest. My hand went to the dagger I kept hidden at my hip, curling my fist around the hilt.

I scanned the darkening forest without moving my head, my eyes darting back and forth between the wide tree trunks, trying to look for shadows that might be unnatural.

"It's only me," came the voice. "Don't worry. The branch was more brittle than it appeared."

My heart squeezed in my chest, a jolt of sorrow and heartache hitting me harder than I'd thought possible.

Lorik.

"Have you been following me this whole time?" I asked, not

bothering to raise my voice, looking in the direction I thought he might've been hiding.

"I just want to make sure you get home safely."

"This is ridiculous," I said, my hand dropping away from the dagger. "Why are you hiding?"

"Because you said you never wanted to see me again."

I pressed my lips together. Yes, he was right about that.

"And you won't—I promise," Lorik continued. "I just wanted you to know that you have nothing to fear in the Black Veil, Marion. I'll always make sure Shades stay away from your path."

I didn't reply, and Lorik said nothing else. I continued on, winding my way home even as my mind raced. I felt flustered, knowing he was watching me, watching *over* me. How long had he done this without me knowing?

And if it thawed a tiny part of my icy heart, I ignored it.

CHAPTER 23

Over the course of the next few days, I found myself taking Lorik's words to heart. Because, it seemed, one part of me still trusted that he would keep me safe, despite what had happened between us.

Gone were the nerves that entered my chest whenever I was beyond Peek's protection. Instead, I felt a fluttering kind of awareness, *knowing* that Lorik was out there, even though I could not see him.

I struggled between trying to ignore that newfound knowledge...and also smoothing down my hair whenever I left my cottage and whenever I entered the Black Veil after my time in Rolara. It was frustratingly ridiculous. How could I be torn between heartbreak over his terrible betrayal while also wanting to look *pretty* for him? I was out of my mind, I'd finally decided, even as I picked out my best dresses that didn't have holes in them.

I still hadn't decided if I'd forgiven Lorik or not. I believed what he'd said. I truly did. And knowing that...I felt it was cold-hearted *not* to forgive him for it. Yes, he had lied to me, used me to get the shadevine-hive heart.

But I also recognized that not only would I want to help my people if they were sick…I would literally do anything to save my *sister*. I would have done *anything* to save her. If I could have traded my life for hers…I would have.

Knowing that, did that change how I felt about what had happened between us in the aftermath? After the heat of the moment had passed and I could reflect on it with calmness and logic?

Of course it did.

However, I just didn't see how it would change anything between us. We'd been doomed from the start. He was a Kelvarian, the Below King's Hunter, and he would never be accepted in the Above world without his magicked glamour—not that he would ever leave his home.

And I could never leave mine. All we would have were stolen moments, like the ones we'd had before, until he was called away again by the magic embedded into his wrist.

And though I'd pushed my own dreams for the future down deep, I realized I wanted a family. I wanted to be loved, and I wanted *to* love. I wanted a partner in this life, one who was kind and caring. I wanted children.

Despite whether I forgave Lorik for what had happened, I didn't think he could give me that.

That night, as I returned from Rolara, all while feeling the heaviness of Lorik's gaze—or at least *imagining* it—I encountered a small package on the threshold of Peek's barrier, sitting on the tree stump near the carved out washing basin.

It was wrapped in the lightest silk I'd ever felt, so smooth and soft that it felt like water slipping through my fingertips when I picked it up.

As the moon began to rise, casting light through the naked branches of the river trees overhead, I unwrapped the white silk to find a smooth stone inside. A warm stone, one etched with what looked like glowing runes. They throbbed like a heartbeat.

I stared down at it in my palm, where it fit neatly within.

"Lorik," I called out.

He didn't reply. A gust of wind picked up, rustling the branches.

"Come out."

I didn't have to wait for long. I steeled myself for the sight of him, but it still felt like a punch in the gut.

He wasn't wearing his glamour anymore. There was no need between us, I supposed. And he was even more handsome than I'd remembered. Or perhaps the time apart had just made me forget.

At his temples, the sides of his long, black hair were pulled away from his face in an intricate braid and pinned at the back of his head. It only put his sharp, wide features on further display. His high cheekbones, his pouting lips, and his cutting jawline. His brows were twin slashes across his face, his eyes tilted at the outer corners like a feline's.

He was wearing a deep maroon vest, the color of human blood, a loose white shirt beneath it. His tight trews looked like suede, but they were supple and molded to his thighs perfectly. I spied the hilt of a silver dagger in his waistband. And as I studied him across the clearing, I watched his wings twitch, flaring once, twice, before he settled them against his back.

Nervous? I wondered.

"What is this?" I asked, though I thought I knew. Lorik's gaze went down to the stone in my hand before it met mine again.

"A magicked stone," he told me. "I've been working on it since… I'm sorry it's taken so long. The runes were tricky to get right."

"It's warm," I commented, my heart beating in my chest.

"I knew you were trying to keep them alive," Lorik murmured, his glowing, beautiful eyes spearing into mine. I was under the impression that he was *drinking* me in, like he feared this might be the last time we would speak. "I thought this would help you."

"A replacement heart for the shadevine hive," I murmured, unsure how I felt about that. "It won't bring the queen back."

"I know," he rasped. "But I thought…I thought this would help. It will stay warm forever. It will never lose its heat. You could keep the hive alive without the queen until the rest…"

"Until they all die out," I finished for him softly. My gaze strayed back to my palm.

He'd done this for me?

I hadn't known he knew runes. A tricky magic, like he'd said, and very few ever mastered it. But they were infinitely more powerful than spells, which could dissipate like a breeze. Runes were permanent. Forever.

The bitter part of me thought it was the least he could do… then I felt ashamed for it.

The other part of me was touched. Another little piece of my icy heart seemed to flaw with the gift. This would keep the hive alive, and I wouldn't have to change out the stone I warmed in the fire multiple times a day. One less thing I'd have to worry about.

Thank you, I thought, but I couldn't say the words. He was the reason why the hive was without a heart, right?

Not him specifically, I reminded myself. Shame reared its head again, and I felt tears prick the backs of my eyes. I was so confused. Everything was muddled and messy, including my ever-changing emotions.

"Don't, Marion," Lorik said, his voice firm and gruff.

Gods, I'd missed his voice. A stab of longing went through me when I remembered hearing it first thing in the mornings, waking up with that voice.

Let's stay in bed all day, he'd tease me, husky and warm. And I remembered how wide my smile had been as I'd pressed my face into his neck, inhaling the comforting scent of his skin.

"Don't what?" I asked.

"Don't thank me," he said, his voice verging on angry. "I can see it. I can hear it. This is the very least I could have done. And still…it will never be enough. Ever. I'm embarrassed that this is the most I can give you."

Silence lapsed between us. Lorik stood as close to Peek's barrier as he could, and yet it felt like the distance was too great.

"I won't thank you," I finally said, looking down at my feet, my gaze flickering between my boots as I deliberated my next words. "But this will be a great help."

Lorik said nothing.

There was a question hanging in the air, one I had thought a dozen times a day.

"Did it work?" I finally asked, glancing back up at him.

Lorik's expression gave nothing away, but I watched as his eyes tracked across my face, like he was memorizing me. My own went to his lips. I could see the tip of one fang indenting his bottom lip, and I swallowed hard, wondering if he longed for the taste of my blood. I wondered if he'd fed since we'd been together…but surely he must've. And why did that thought make a prick of hot jealousy spear through my belly? Of imagining Lorik with another woman? Another Kelvarian, who was perhaps better suited to his life than I was?

"The spell seems to have stopped new Shades being created," he told me. "No new reports have come in."

"Good," I said quietly. "And your…sister?"

Lorik swallowed, his throat bobbing, his right wing lifting slightly. "The sorceress said it might take time."

My gut clenched. Which meant that no, she wasn't recovered.

"But we are hopeful," he said. "Other Kelvarians have recovered swiftly. More do every day. I haven't lost hope for Thela. She's strong. She *will* recover."

I nodded. "I hope so."

The stone beat in my hand—a part of Lorik's magic, rare and powerful, and it felt oddly intimate to have it in my possession.

When I began to turn away, Lorik said, "Marion."

I looked over my shoulder at him. There were so many words perched on the edge of his tongue. I could see them. I could *hear* them, just like Lorik had said to me earlier. Maybe our connection *was* a magical thing…and a part of me wished it wasn't.

Lorik opened his lips. Then he shook his head, huffing out a sharp breath as his gaze strayed to the earth beneath his feet.

Then he straightened his shoulders, meeting my eyes again. Whatever brief vulnerability that had been evident was long gone.

"The Below King would like to extend his deepest appreciation for your help," Lorik said quietly. "He is in your debt. We all are. If you ever have a favor to ask, he will personally see to it upheld."

My lips parted.

A favor? I had no need of one. There was nothing I wanted, except to go back in time and lie in Lorik's arms once more, memory erased and ignorantly blissful.

Besides…I was in the Above world. What use would I—

A thought occurred to me.

"You said Merec's debt was to a Sev—to a Kelvarian," I said.

Lorik blinked. "Yes, that's right."

"Has the debt been repaid?" I wondered.

"Not fully," Lorik murmured. "He still has another five years on the contract."

"Then I would ask the Below King to forgive whatever debt Merec owes," I said. "That is what I want."

Lorik lowered his chin in understanding. He brought a hand to run it along his horn, and I remembered the feel of the black bone beneath my own fingertips. A pang went through me as I mentally counted the steps between us.

"I will relay your message to him," Lorik said. "He will see it done."

I nodded. Then, knowing there was nothing else to say, I turned.

"Marion."

I stilled but didn't look at him again. I merely waited.

The words came, a quiet confession.

"I miss you, little witch," he told me softly, his voice hushed in the quiet of the evening. It sounded almost reverent. A murmured prayer. "Even when I'm in the Below...all I want is to be here with you."

Tears filled my eyes, making my vision go blurry. I tried to blink them away quickly, but there was a rawness in Lorik's voice that haunted me. His words replayed over and over in my head.

"I don't know if you can ever forgive me, Marion," he continued. "I don't know if I even want you to because I don't know if I can ever forgive myself for betraying you."

My brow furrowed, staring at my night garden next to my cottage, the trellis entrance withering with the cold.

"But please know...I am deeply sorry, Marion."

Whatever I heard in his voice—whatever pained, terrible thing I heard—it made me turn to meet his eyes. His lips pressed when he saw the tears glimmering in my gaze, and he took a stuttered step forward, as if he couldn't help it, before Peek's barrier pushed him back.

I didn't even care if he saw me crying.

Holding my eyes, he said, "I am deeply sorry for betraying your trust. But I am not sorry for everything else."

I frowned.

"Because I will hold those moments with me forever, little witch. I cannot bring myself to regret *any* moment that I spent with you. Even when you were pulling an arrow out from my shoulder. Because it meant you were close to me. And only in those moments did I feel like I could finally breathe."

My lips parted.

"I know you have no reason to trust me," he continued. "I have given you none. But I would give you my blood oath right here and now if it meant erasing any doubt in your mind about the way I feel about you."

My mind raced. A blood oath? He would be forever bound to it. Just like the one he'd made to the Below King, like the one I'd made to the Healers' Guild.

"I regret that I hurt you. For the rest of my life, I will regret that," he said. "But I do not know if I have the will to say goodbye to you, Marion. Every moment away from you has been agony. Every moment in the Below has felt like a lifetime. It will break my soul if I have to say goodbye to you...but if that's truly what you want, I will respect that. I swear it to you."

I bit my lip, trying to keep it from quivering. Maybe I was weak...but I didn't want that, did I? Maybe I hadn't known it before, but actually *hearing* him say it? That hurt even more. Imagining *never* seeing him again. Never looking upon his face, never seeing that wide grin and the sly twinkle in his eyes when he teased me. Never hearing his voice, never feeling his gentle touch across my shoulders, my back, my abdomen, my hips...

Gods, that hurt.

"But," Lorik said, a tone entering his voice after he observed me process that information, "if there is a part of you that could forgive me even the smallest bit, if there is a part of you that still believes in this, in *us*..."

I inhaled a shaky breath that sounded like a small sob.

"I'll be here," he finished. "I'll always be here, Marion. Take as much time as you need to make that decision."

Lorik blew out a short breath, holding my gaze...and then began to walk away, back into the shadowy tree line of the Black Veil. Would he return to the Below to see his sister? Or would he patrol the forest for Shades, protecting his realm and ours?

"Lorik," I called out, quickly.

He turned so fast one would think a Shade had crept up behind him.

I didn't want to give him the wrong impression, but I wanted to be honest with him too. I didn't want to swallow down the words I felt rising in my throat.

"I miss you too," I said.

The edge of his lips curved in a gentle smile. He didn't say anything else. I knew he would give me time to make my decision.

"Be careful in there," I said next, finally turning away, the rune stone hot in my hand as I gripped it hard.

"I always am, little witch."

CHAPTER 24

Another week passed, and the path into Rolara was now covered in snow and icicles. The Black Veil in winter had always been beautiful. Peaceful and quiet…but lonely. I'd never felt the loneliness more as I trekked each day into the village. While I'd come to enjoy Rolara, to nod and wave and smile at familiar faces that were becoming even more familiar to me by the day, it always reminded me that I was alone.

Lately, the walls of my cottage had seemed too close. Lately, I'd had a difficult time finding sleep, dreaming of Lorik, missing him so much that it physically ached in my breast.

I'd only seen him a handful times throughout the week, though I'd always felt his presence near. We'd spoken briefly, in conversations that always felt too short—but just long enough to realize that we were both miserable.

Thela hadn't recovered fully though she continued to improve every day. Two days ago, she'd begun to eat again, and I'd seen the emotion on Lorik's face, the shimmering in his eyes, to know how much that had relieved him. I hadn't realized how bad it had been, but he'd confessed that she'd been on the brink of death, even with the help of the spell.

Life was continuing on, in the Above and the Below, apparently.

So why couldn't we? Why did I feel so stuck?

I huffed out a deep sigh, keeping my ears perked for Lorik as I walked home from Rolara in the darkness. I'd begun to bring my Halo orb with me, and it floated in front of me, illuminating my path, twinkling off icicles and patches of snow as my winter boots crunched through it.

It had been a hard day. The Healers' Guild had lost an older patient, one whose body had simply given out. His name had been Povar. Just last week, I'd given him a salve for his aching joints and he'd made the trek back to the guild hall the following day just to thank me. He'd had a kind smile and a warm soul.

And today...he was just gone.

"What are you thinking of, little witch?"

I took in a deep breath through my nostrils, and I was surprised by the sense of comfort and relief I felt the moment I heard his voice, funneling its way to me like a warm, summer wind.

I'd almost made it to the cottage. Lorik was leaning against the trunk of a river tree, dressed in a fur-lined long-sleeved shirt and a thick, intricate vest with a beautifully stitched pattern. His pants were a dark blue, the color of midnight, and his black boots were tipped in silver metal.

I was used to the sight of him now, his features no longer suppressed by his magicked glamour. Even his eyes glowed more brightly.

"How easy is it for you to use glamour?" I wondered, stopping in front of him.

In an instant, the Lorik I'd known was before me. Softer, more delicate features like an Allavari. Even the broadness of his shoulders and the width of his chest seemed to shrink, and I wondered how I couldn't have felt it when we'd been intimate.

But magic was powerful. And I'd always known Lorik's was greater than any I'd ever seen.

Are all Kelvarians this powerful? I wondered.

"Do you prefer me like this?" he asked. His voice was the same, though I thought it matched his true face better, now that I knew both.

"No," I answered. It was my honest answer. "Because it's not truly you. It's what you think others need to see."

Lorik dropped the glamour like he was lowering a shield. His eyes were even more vibrant against the snowy backdrop, like he'd been made for winter.

"What were you thinking of, Marion?" he asked again. "You look upset."

I sighed. My eyes went to my cottage behind me. Dark and empty and cold. And for some reason, the thought of stoking up a fire inside by myself tonight felt like the most horrible thing.

"An older Allavari male died today at the guild hall," I told him. "Povar. I didn't know him well, but he was kind to me. And I don't know… I feel…I feel…"

Lost.

"I'm sorry, Marion," Lorik murmured. "Death is never an easy thing. It doesn't matter if you knew him well or not. You still cared about him."

I swallowed, tugging my shawl closer around my shoulders.

"Will you…" I started. "Would you like to come in for some tea?"

The silence that stretched felt charged with electricity, but I didn't walk back my words. I wondered if that was why Lorik took so long to answer—because he was waiting for me to regret the question and change my mind.

Only I never did.

"Yes," he finally replied. "I would."

I nodded and turned, my heart thumping in my chest. Lorik

followed me, his footsteps nearly silent in the snow. He stopped, however, at Peek's boundary, and without hesitation, I took his hand and pulled him over.

The heat of his skin felt shocking and welcome. He didn't drop my hand. He threaded his fingers in between mine, and I felt my shoulders relax.

The chill of my cottage was startling. Lorik released my hand as the Halo orb floated into the front room, casting sharp shadows across the wall from the furniture. I went to light my candles, and without me asking, Lorik sparked the fire in the hearth, his movements practiced and sure. All the wood he'd chopped for me had been used up, and I realized it had been over three weeks since he'd last been inside the cottage.

When the fire roared to life and the candles had been lit, golden light filled the front room. There was pawing at the door, and I let Peek inside. My *braydus* slinked into the room slowly, shaking the snow off his fur. His head turned to regard Lorik carefully. Then he huffed out a sharp breath through his nostrils, ignored Lorik completely—at least that was what he wanted Lorik to believe—and went to eat when I filled his bowl with raw meat.

"He still hates me, I see," Lorik commented.

"Peek doesn't like anyone."

"He's protective of you," he replied. "That's all that matters. You couldn't have a better companion. I feel better knowing that."

I regarded Lorik across the room. If I'd thought he'd filled my cottage before, he made it seem ten times smaller now.

Ice was melting off my shawl, and I unwrapped it, hanging it by the door. Unbuttoning my thick overcoat next—one that needed a few holes to be patched. I was a little embarrassed by the state of my clothes, especially next to Lorik. And with the extra money coming in from my shifts at the guild hall, repairing the majority of my wardrobe and investing in new winter clothes was my first priority.

"Let me get the kettle on the fire," he said, and behind me, I heard him prepping it. My heart was racing. It was tense and a little awkward, like we both didn't know what to do with ourselves, where to place our bodies in the room…

And yet I didn't regret asking him inside. Having him here was like a nice memory. And a part of me wanted to forget it all —forget the way he'd hurt me—and just move forward.

When Lorik set the kettle over the fire, I turned. Steam was rising off him as he lingered by the flames, and it took me a moment to realize he was using magic to dry his clothes. When they were, he pushed up his sleeves and then settled down into his usual place at the table.

"What's it like in the Below?" I asked quietly. Lorik looked at me sharply, blinking once. "Unless you're not allowed to tell me."

His jaw tightened. "No more secrets, Marion. I'll tell you whatever you wish to know."

"Then tell me what it's like—where you live."

"Allavari think the Below is a hellscape of demons and fire and dark magic and twisted souls," Lorik said, quirking his lips up in a dry smile. "It couldn't be more opposite. The Below is more beautiful than anything you've ever seen."

My brow furrowed.

"I live in a place called Aeysara. The Below King's bright city. I was born there, raised there. And like the Above world, there are countless villages spread across our land, ranging from small strongholds to sprawling towns that stretch for miles and miles. We truly do not know the boundaries of the Below. Over centuries, we've had scouts try to find the edges of our world, but we've never found them. The truth is that we call it the Below and this place the Above…but sometimes I wonder if it's the opposite. The Below isn't actually *below*. And the Above isn't actually above us. They are just two different realms of Allavar, bound by the portal in the Black Veil. But in the Below…the magic there is powerful. It's steeped in it."

I took all this in with rapt fascination.

"And when you come up to the Above world," I began, "do you feel the lack of magic here?"

"Yes," he said quietly. "I feel depleted here if I stay too long."

I pressed my lips together, thinking as much.

"But it's a small price to pay," he added.

I sucked in a breath as I looked at him. What was he saying?

Lorik leaned forward, his forearms sliding across the flat surface of my wood table. Gingerly, I took a seat across from him, ignoring my icy feet in my winter boots or the wet marks I'd tracked along my stone floor, which would dry as the cottage heated.

"Is it winter there now?" I asked. "In Aeysara?"

"No," he said. "Our seasons do not change. The first time I saw snow, felt it…it was shocking. The cold, the rain, the heat during the warm season—we don't feel that in the Below. We have ancient spells in place to keep our lands temperate, fueled partly by the Below King's magic."

"That must be nice," I said quietly.

"Sometimes," he said. "But I've grown quite fond of rain and storms and never quite knowing what the day will bring. There is an excitement and unpredictability in it. I have this fantasy…"

I held my breath as I waited for him to speak.

"Of us," he murmured, catching my eyes, "in another life. Where we wake to a storm, and we have so much to get done that day. Wood to be chopped, provisions to buy from the village, the garden needing tending, and your potions to brew. And the storm comes, and we just decide to forget all of it. To stay warm in bed and listen to the rain on the roof."

My chest gave a sharp pang as longing went through me. Another life, he'd said. Was something like that still possible in this one? When he'd said himself that his magic slowly depleted every time he came to the Above?

"That's what you dream about?" I whispered.

"Among other things, yes," he said, swallowing. He seemed embarrassed as he shifted in his chair, as if he hadn't meant to confess those things. "But…anyway, no, it's not winter in the Below. It likely never will be."

There were so many questions. Questions I'd wondered in the weeks we'd been apart. Questions that seemed too vast that I couldn't even think of a single one to voice now. It was too overwhelming.

"Don't," Lorik's gentle voice came. Could he read me so clearly? "We have as much time as you'll give me, Marion."

Meaning…he'd wait for me until I asked him not to. Meaning…he would always be here until I asked him to leave.

I choked out a small sob, torn between a smile and tears. I pressed my hands to my face before I raked them back into my hair, pushing back my unruly auburn waves as I breathed deeply.

"I…I've been thinking of offering my glowflies to the Healers' Guild," I confessed. "Of transferring the hives and uprooting all the plants. Of…of leaving my cottage and moving back to the village. Or maybe not even Rolara. Maybe elsewhere in Allavar. I don't know."

The words tumbled out of me in a rush.

"And the crazy thing is that I don't know that I *want* to," I said in the quiet, the only sound the crackling fire. "I don't know if it's just because of everything that happened. If I'm a little heartbroken, a little lonely, or if I just need a change."

Lorik frowned.

"The Black Veil helped me heal after Aysia. But I also realize that I've used it as a shield since," I said. "I've just been a little lost lately. And I don't know why I'm telling you this when there's a million other things to ask you. But this week…whenever you've asked me how I've been, a part of me just wants to scream all this. I don't want to hide it anymore."

"Marion…" he said softly.

I sniffed, lowering my hands away from the sides of my head, and my hair fell back into place. The water began to boil over the hearth, and I made a move to stand.

"Leave it," Lorik told me, catching my hand quickly across the table. "I want to talk about *this*."

Slowly, I lowered back down into my seat.

"Tell me," he said.

"You hurt me," I whispered. Lorik breathed in slowly and deeply at the words. Was that relief on his face? "You hurt me real bad, Lorik Ravael. But I forgive you for it."

That made his brows furrow. Did he *want* me to be angry with him forever? Because he thought he deserved it?

"I forgive you for it. Because I understand why you had to do it. I can understand how there would be no choice in something like that. I just wish…I just wish it hadn't hurt so much."

"I told you before, Marion," he said, his voice gruff. "My feelings for you were never a lie. I never had to pretend with you. The lie was just…everything else. The circumstances of how we met. And what I needed from you."

"Looking back on it, I think you were always trying to tell me," I said. "I remember the conversations we had about perception and reality, if I believed that there were things in the universe that would upend everything I knew. You were talking about the Kelvarians, about Severs and Shades, about Allavari, about you. I see that now. I see it so clearly. And I always think about that last night, when we were bathing together and you told me your sister was sick."

Lorik's jaw tightened, his thumb stroking over the back of my hand.

"Were you trying to tell me then?" I asked.

"Yes," he said softly. "I just didn't know *how*, Marion. Everything was piling up around me. The lies, my deepening feelings for you, my duty to my people, to my family. I had to weigh everything so carefully. Because truthfully, I was running out of time. It was the one thing I had little left of. Every moment I spent with you, the darkness was spreading more and more in the Below, slowly turning innocent lives into Shades. We had no idea if the hive heart would even work—only the word of a sorceress. Even knowing that, even with all the pressure from the Below, I didn't want to hurt you. I didn't want you to think that…that I was only with you because I *needed* something from you. I *did*, but it was more than that."

"I know," I said softly. "It was an impossible decision. And there was really one choice. I understand."

"It doesn't change the fact that I hurt you," Lorik murmured. "And I hate that I had to. It's the worst thing I've ever done."

The honest words hung in the air. We stared at each other across the table, and for once, the distance between us didn't seem so great, so insurmountable.

The kettle kept whistling over the fire, and I squeezed his hand as I stood from the table. He let me go this time, and I prepped our tea in silence before sliding the cup over to him, taking my seat again.

Steam curled from the cup as I took the first small sip and peered over the rim at him.

I watched as he reached toward his cup, catching sight of a mark on his wrist I'd never seen before.

"What's that?" I asked, my cup hitting the table with a loud thud. "Are you being called to the Below?"

"No," he said, hiding the mark when he curled his hand around his cup. "It's nothing."

"I thought we agreed no more secrets."

Lorik's lips pressed together, and he gave a self-deprecating smirk. "You're right."

Then with a small moment of hesitation, he slid his wrist across the table and showed me.

Whether made by ink or magic, it was an intricate black symbol, resembling a shield, though at its very center there were words written upon it. In Kelvarian? I didn't recognize it.

I got a strange feeling as I looked at it, and I met Lorik's eyes. "What is it?"

His nostrils flared. He studied me carefully and then said, "It's a crime mark."

Suddenly, I understood what he meant. The Shade…Lorik had looked at his wrist after he'd killed him. *Crimes*, he'd said when he'd seen the markings. I remembered the flash of disgust I'd seen on his face, and I wondered what crimes the Shade had committed.

Dread pooled in my belly.

"What does it say?"

"Oath breaker," he told me, taking his wrist back and tugging his sleeve down to shield it from my sight. He picked up his cup in that hand and took a long swig of his hot tea.

"Your blood oath," I whispered, the color draining from my face. The one I'd forced him to break. "Tell me what it means for you."

"Kelvarians are held to laws bound in honor. Every crime is marked on our skin like a tally. A shameful history, for all to see. Theft is one marking. Murder is three. Every Kelvarian is only allowed three markings, three chances…then you are sentenced to death or the land of the Shades by public trial."

Horror clawed up my throat. "What?"

"It seems strict perhaps to an Allavari," he murmured, "but the system works for the Below."

"But you're…you're the Below King's Hunter," I said.

"Even the Below King is not above Kelvarian law," he told me. "Even the Below King has a crime mark of his own."

My lips parted.

"And…and how many more do you get before…"

"Oath breaker," he repeated, staring down at the now-concealed mark, "normally counts as two markings against me. But mine was in service to the Below King, and so it was judged during the trial to only count as one. I have two chances left before…"

Tears sprung into my eyes. "It's not fair," I whispered.

Lorik took my hand again. "Nothing ever is, little witch. This isn't your fault."

"It is!" I said angrily. "How can you say it's not?"

"Because I knew that it was very likely I would need to break my blood oath when the Below King tasked me with this. I went into this knowing that. You were never going to give me the hive heart with no explanation, and I didn't want to lie to you anymore, Marion."

"I wish you had!"

Gods…*death*? Or the land of the Shades—whatever that meant! Just the thought of Lorik no longer being a part of this world made mine feel like it was falling apart.

And that should've been my first clue that I was falling in love with the Kelvarian male who'd stolen a lot more than the hive heart.

"I've gone this long without a crime mark, Marion," he said. "By the trial's mercy, it is not so dire as it could've been."

"Because you helped saved your people," I whispered. "You shouldn't have been marked at all."

"No, *you* helped save my people," he said. "Don't forget that."

I scoffed. It seemed like a small thing compared to this, and it made me realize that there was so much more happening beneath the surface, things I still couldn't anticipate or see.

But that's life, I realized. You either swayed with it like a current or you fought it until it drowned you.

"I'm sorry," I said quietly.

"Don't apologize to me," Lorik said, frowning.

It was then I knew he still hadn't forgiven himself, even though *I* had.

"I'm still sorry," I said, squeezing his hand. "I can't help how I feel."

And I knew that the mark brought him shame. He would carry it for the rest of his life—a constant reminder of what he'd done, even though he'd only wanted to help with people, his sister.

It wasn't fair.

But nothing ever was. Lorik had been right about that.

CHAPTER 25

It was market day once more. A whole moon cycle had passed since the last, the evening that Veras had told me that Lorik was a Sever—a Kelvarian from the Below. The evening I'd learned the truth.

It felt like a lifetime ago in some ways. Yet it had passed in the blink of an eye.

But much had changed since. I marveled that I'd gone to countless market days in the last ten years and each one had felt the same. This one? It couldn't feel any different.

For once, I smiled and waved at the vendors as I passed, many I'd spoken to in the village at least once in the last month. Eymaris came up to my stall to chat as I unpacked my potions, all healing salves and potions to help with sleep since the death needle crop had been bountiful this season.

And during the market itself, Griffel and Salladar and Winnand, families of patients I'd treated, shopkeepers I'd sent business to, and even fellow healers from the guild all passed by to talk, looking over my potions or dropping off their old bottles to me from the previous market days, which I appreciated. Many brought me gifts—food from one of the vendors, a bundle of winter flowers, a neatly wrapped package of thick socks. I was surprised and touched by the generosity.

I found that the market day flew by because of the people. The friends I'd begun to make in Rolara. Everyone seemed in great spirits—not even the snowfall and the icy chill in the air could dampen it. The music seemed more vibrant, traveling across the cold air more swiftly, and the heat and press of bodies felt more welcome.

And I realized that *I'd* done this. I'd created this for me. This sense of belonging in Rolara. This sense of community.

If I'd hidden myself away in the Black Veil this last month, like I always had, this market day wouldn't have felt so special.

By the time it was growing dark, my throat hurt from talking and laughing with passing villagers and neighboring vendors. Not even the sight of Veras dampened my spirits. I'd nodded at him without prompting, and he'd tipped his chin down, going on his way.

And just as I began to pack up my cart, I caught sight of Lorik.

My breath seized in my lungs, anticipation giving my heart a rough jolt.

I wondered how long he'd been watching me, but he was leaning back against the apothecary shop, his usual place during market days, and his eyes were pinned on me, a small smile playing across his lips.

For a moment, it was like we'd gone back in time. To before I'd even known his name. He had his glamour on, of course, since we were in the village, but a part of me wished I could see *him*. His true self. I wished the others could too.

I saw the long looks cast his way, but he paid people no mind as they skirted around him. He was only looking at me, his arms crossed over his chest, his pose relaxed and at ease.

After that night in my cottage, I'd seen him twice more and only very briefly. He'd been called back to the Below. We'd left *us* up in the air, an unspoken thing after what we'd discussed. About his crime marking, about the Below, about my thoughts of giving up my cottage.

There was still so much to discuss, so much to figure out—how this would even work. If it *could* even work.

Especially since I knew Lorik still hadn't forgiven himself. Forgiveness had always been a difficult thing for me, given my past with Veras. With Lorik…I'd found forgiveness came easily. The same couldn't be said for him.

When I was finally alone, Lorik pushed away from the building of the apothecary and strode over to me, his footsteps strong and certain, and I counted every single one because they matched my heartbeat.

"Popular little witch," he murmured, his voice dipped low so the neighboring vendor couldn't eavesdrop. "I've been trying to get you alone all evening."

I wanted to reach out and hold him. I wanted to feel his arms around me once more, but the only touch we'd had in the last few weeks had been when we'd held one another's hands at my cottage. There was a barrier we hadn't passed yet, a line neither of us had crossed.

Would tonight be the night we would?

I hope so, I couldn't help but wish. I'd done a lot of thinking these last few weeks. Too much. I was tired of thinking, I'd decided. Lorik had been correct about me all those weeks ago. I *was* driven by logic, and for once, I just wanted to do what felt *right*.

And to me, Lorik felt right. Despite everything.

The Halo lights were beginning to flicker on in the village, making it glow in the distance. My own orb was weaving around us, casting shadows across our faces as I tucked my tablecloth back into my cart, laden with the gifts I'd received today. For once, it would be nearly as heavy lugging back to my cottage as it was into the market.

"You've been here all this time?" I asked, suddenly shy.

He nodded.

"Are you...are you back for a little while?"

Lorik's lips turned up. It felt strange now, looking at his glamour when I knew the truth. What had Veras said? Power was knowledge. It peeled the veil away from your eyes.

Now I understood what he'd meant. I would never see the world the way I had before.

"Yes," he said. "My sister...she's awake."

My breath hitched. "Really?"

He nodded, and I saw the relief glide over his face, as if he couldn't believe it himself. "It's remarkable. Truly," he said. "That's why I was called back. That day, she just...woke up. It's like it never happened. She's back. Thela came back."

I rounded the table and, without hesitation, wrapped my arms around him. I didn't care if people were watching. I didn't care if they would whisper or gossip about us. I only cared about Lorik and the catch I'd heard in his voice. And I thought...*I want to meet his sister one day.*

Would that even be possible?

Lorik's arms went tight around me, and I pressed my face into his chest, feeling the hard thump of his heart against my cheek. Maybe this would be what he needed to help him forgive himself. His sister. Me.

We'd taken this slow, hadn't we? We'd felt one another out, tiptoeing around the idea after Lorik's necessary betrayal. But it had been long enough.

All I knew was that it had felt like a lifetime without him already. I didn't know if I could go another day.

"I'm happy for you," I said quietly, inhaling his scent deeply. His vest was luxuriously soft and supple, crafted by an expert hand. Our lives were so vastly different, but for the first time, I didn't care. It didn't matter. "Happy for her and your family."

"Thank you," he whispered. And I knew he was thanking me for more than my words.

"I told you already," I said, "the hive heart seems small in comparison now. Don't thank me for that."

"I will *always* thank you. Because it wasn't an easy thing. You sacrificed something you cared deeply for, something that was a constant in your life for years, for people you don't even know."

His words ruffled my hair, and I closed my eyes against him, feeling warm and safe in his arms. Because the truth was that I would always have a scar of my own, just like the crime marking on his inner wrist. The shadevine queen's sting would always ache, a perpetual reminder of what I'd needed to do.

"Let's make a deal," I suggested.

Lorik pulled back, running his eyes over my face carefully, hearing something in my tone that tightened the muscles in his body. "Oh?"

I drew in a deep breath, my heart pounding.

"I think we should put what happened behind us," I said.

His brows drew together.

"I—I want to move forward, Lorik," I told him, feeling the words clog up my throat, but I'd been feeling the truth of them for some time. "With you. If you still want that."

His eyes glowed through his glamour before he could conceal their light.

"I miss you," I whispered.

"Marion—"

"I miss you a lot," I admitted. "I think we've both been a little miserable without each other, and I don't want to regret anything. Not with you. I don't want to regret not seeing what this could be just because we don't know *what* could be. And I know there's so much to figure out…but I—"

Lorik's lips were on mine before I could utter another word. And I didn't care that we were giving the lingering vendors a show and there would be talk in the village tomorrow morning. I wrapped my arms around Lorik's neck and kissed him back, having missed his taste and the heat of his lips on mine.

I never wanted it to end.

But when it did, he murmured against my lips, "I'm a little in love with you, Marion."

The words made my chest squeeze, and I couldn't help the wobbly smile that crossed my face.

"I'm a little in love with you too, Lorik Ravael," I whispered back.

His lips brushed against mine, soft and sweet and slow. And I thought my heart would burst from my chest in relief and happiness. I felt like I could float high above Rolara with his kiss.

"If that's the case," he began, "I have something to ask you."

"Yes?"

"Would you join me for an Allavari ale at Grimstone's tonight?"

My laugh was soft, and the wide smile splitting my face actually hurt.

"When you order one, just call it an ale," I teased. "And yes, I will. But only if you promise to steal a kiss from me in one of the back booths."

Lorik's laugh felt like a victory. I hadn't heard it in so long, I hadn't realized how much I'd missed it.

"I promise, little witch."

EPILOGUE

Two moon cycles later...

"Lorik," I chided, struggling to conceal my smile when his hands squeezed my backside. "You're being very distracting."

"*You* are distracting, little witch," he murmured, pressing his hips against me, his lips brushing against my ear. I could feel the outline of his cock against his loose trews, hard and warm. And I let out a breathy moan when he nibbled on the column of my throat, a frustrated groan meeting my ears.

He squeezed my backside again.

"Later," he promised.

"Later," I agreed, stepping away, a little more flushed than I'd been before. "Just a few more riverberries. And maybe some willowroot moss if we can find it."

"I haven't seen any willowroot lately," Lorik commented, watching me as I reached down to pluck a few plump berries off the vines growing close to the river bank. "Last I saw any was to the north, near the Massadians. I'll snag some for you if I ever see it again."

"Thank you," I commented, reaching out to run my hand down his arm. Warm, hard, and strong beneath my fingertips. A flash of desire speared through me, thinking of our lovemaking that very morning—the driving pound of his hips, his wings giving him momentum, getting him as deep as possible.

I bit my lip.

"Ahh," Lorik murmured, his eyes narrowing on something in the distance. He began walking, and I trailed behind him after snagging a few more riverberries for the scones I would make tomorrow morning.

"What do you see?"

Lorik, I'd discovered, had much better vision, especially in the Black Veil. Much better senses overall truthfully. He could hear a critter half a mile away scurrying up the trunk of a tree, smell the riverberries when they ripened from my cottage, and see a Shade in the darkness where I could not.

"Star grass. I'll get some for Peek," he replied.

"Still trying to bribe him?" I teased, wiping my stained fingers on the thick cloth I'd brought with me.

"One day, he will adore me," Lorik vowed, flashing me a mischievous grin. "Didn't you see him last night? He brushed up against my leg. On purpose."

"Yes, I did," I replied, an amused smile tugging on my lips at the excitement I heard in his tone.

Peek was beginning to warm to Lorik's presence, now that it was nearly constant in the cottage. But my *braydus* had a mean streak, I'd begun to learn. Once, Lorik had brought him a braised Massadian bird leg from the market, not knowing that Peek *detested* Massadian birds. As punishment, Peek hadn't allowed Lorik past his barrier around the cottage. Lorik had needed to call out for me, and I'd had to pull him through.

Though I'd scolded Peek afterward—and though it had never

happened since—I always got the sense that Peek had been infinitely pleased with himself, and Lorik had grumbled about it for days.

But…now there seemed to be a truce between them. Peek especially liked Lorik's gifts for him, though Lorik was always sure to ask me if Peek would like them first.

The patch of star grass was a bright blue, shimmering in the darkness that was beginning to stretch through the Black Veil, slowly like a thick fog. I never worried being out here so late. Not with Lorik. I enjoyed the moonlight, the quiet. It relaxed me. And if a branch snapped in the distance or I heard the movement of slow, shuffling feet, I knew to trust in my male's instincts. I knew to trust that he would protect me if we ever encountered something more dangerous.

Just when Lorik was reaching down, his breath inhaled sharply, and a small stab of disappointment went through my belly.

"So soon?" I asked, looking at his wrist when he began to pluck the star grass in solid clumps from the damp earth. There I saw the summons, like opal-colored ink on his skin. He'd just returned from the Below three days before.

"It can wait until tomorrow," he promised me, checking the mark.

"Are you sure?" I asked, biting my lip.

"We discussed it, yes?" Lorik said, giving me a small smile when he stood, fresh star grass clamped in his palm. He deposited them in the basket hanging from my arm and stole a quick kiss, his arm threading around my waist.

I nodded, ease slowly loosening my shoulders.

He meant the Below King when he said *we*.

Shortly after we'd made the decision to give *us* a chance, together, Lorik had told me that he would leave the Below to be with me.

And though the gesture had nearly brought me to tears, it

had made me realize that I didn't want him to do that. Not for me. The Below *was* his home...what he loved—where his family, his duty lay. It would be more difficult, yes. Lorik would be called away at odd hours of the day and night, depending on the severity and urgency of the summons. Most times, I wouldn't know when I would see him next.

But we'd made adjustments. He sent me messages through magicked birds that would disappear in a puff of silver smoke when they delivered his letters. Letters of when he would be back, assuring me that he was safe, that he loved me, that he couldn't wait until I was in his arms once more—all written in midnight-blue ink with his certain, steady hand.

He'd spoken with the Below King, who didn't want to lose Lorik as his Hunter. And so, agreements had been made between them. Smaller scouting duties, both in the Below and Above worlds, would be passed to others. Lorik would only be called to the Below for council meetings, trials, and more important matters that the Below King didn't trust others to handle.

And so, Lorik was free to live in both the Below and the Above.

Though there was a pressing thought that was becoming louder and louder in my mind as the days dragged on without him.

"Lorik."

"Hmm?"

"Do you think..." I trailed off, watching him straighten to regard me. I gave him a nervous smile. "Do you think that I would be welcome in the Below? One day?" I added quickly.

Lorik studied me, and then his eyes glowed brighter.

Then he leaned forward, pressing a soft, gentle kiss to my lips. And he stayed there. His tongue stroked mine, his hand wrapped around my waist, holding me to him. It was a warm embrace. Loving. He made me feel so incredibly safe and wanted.

"Yes," he murmured finally. "You would be most welcome, Marion."

"Really?" I asked.

"My sister has been asking to meet you."

My stomach zinged with sudden nerves…but also delight. "Really?"

Lorik smiled. His thumb brushed my cheek. "But it's not an easy decision—I know that."

"But like with everything we do," I said softly, "we can figure it out. As long as I'm with you and you're with me, that's all that matters, right?"

Lorik grinned. And it was the most beautiful thing I'd ever seen. Even more than my glowflies at midnight in the garden. Even more than a pretty moonrise or the lakelight leaves when they turned color during the harvest season.

"I love you so much, little witch," he rasped.

I smiled back. Those words never failed to bring a flurry of wonderment to my chest.

"I love you too," I whispered, pressing my lips to his, my basket full from our foraging in the Black Veil.

"Let's head back," he suggested, taking my hand in his. "It's getting late."

But on our return to the cottage, as darkness fell and the glow of the moon was shrouded behind clouds…Lorik stilled on the path, his eyes trained on something in the distance, to the west.

"What is it?"

"I don't know," he said, brow furrowed. "Follow close."

We trekked toward whatever it was that Lorik had spied in the forest, and the closer we came, the more light I saw. Blue light, slightly silver, emanating from a hollowed-out circle in the trunk of a tree, high above our heads.

I gasped when I spied the familiar crawling vines looping and swirling their way up the trunk.

"Is that…?" Lorik trailed off, his voice hushed.

"Yes," I breathed, turning to face him wide-eyed. I laughed in disbelief. "My gods."

Shadevines, with their thick, flat, velvety leaves, wound up the tree like a welcome embrace. And in the hollow of the trunk, I watched a shadevine glowfly dart out, landing on a nearby leaf. Then another. Another.

A shadevine hive in the Black Veil.

Lorik squeezed my hand, his palm warm and strong.

And I smiled.

KEEP READING FOR A BONUS PREQUEL SHORT STORY FROM LORIK'S POV

This bonus short story includes a fully immersive audiobook. With a multicast of talented narrators, original music, and sound effects, it's a unique and fun experience…and we encourage you to listen as you read along:

THE BELOW KING'S HUNTER

A PREQUEL SHORT STORY TO *THE MIDNIGHT ARROW*

AUDIOBOOK CAST

Marcio Catalano as Lorik

Angelina Rocca as Marion

Aaron Shedlock as the Below King

Stephanie Nemeth Parker as Rysana

Victoria Connolly as Thela

Sean Orlikowski as Silas

PRODUCED BY ATLANTIS AUDIO

THE BELOW KING'S HUNTER

An east wind pushed the drizzle in such a way that it flurried like snow. A strong gust would make the droplets sliver and dance. Then the wind would calm and the village of Rolara would appear picturesque, a frozen landscape against the darkness of the Black Veil forest, standing tall like a sentinel at its side.

It was market day. The moon cycle had begun anew, its silvery light like a timekeeper for the villagers below it, a dial turning. Tables lined the pathway into the center of the village. Wrinkled, colorful cloths were pressed to their surfaces to hide the cracking, warped wood beneath them. That day, there were twenty-three vendors but only twenty-two tables. One vendor didn't bother, selling his skewers of Massadian bird right off the firepit he'd built in front of himself. Crouched down in the muddy earth, he wiped the drizzle from his eyes with the edge of the tattered sheet he was using to protect his glowing embers and flickering flames.

I found Rolara to be a sleepy little place. Old. Dull. It wasn't beautiful. Traveling along the main road, one might pass the village by, wrinkling their nose. Olimara, the larger village on the other side of the Black Veil, boasted intricate building facades and watch towers chiseled and carved by only the best Allavari stone masons. Their archives rivaled the capital's, drawing scholars and masters from all over Allavar. Its wealth apparent from the pristine condition of its cobble-lined streets and the nature and dress of its inhabitants, for only the wealthy could afford to live there. Situated along the coast, Olimara could access trading ports—imports and exports—that Rolara could not.

Stuck. Sometimes Rolara felt abandoned. Gridlocked next to the Black Veil. Olimara thought this village was cursed. Most in Allavar believed the same.

But to me, Rolara was charming. There was a peace and a quietness here that I craved, that eased a frenetic pulse in my chest. It was a simple life here. It intrigued me.

There was a figure emerging from the Black Veil, making me straighten against the stone wall of the apothecary behind me, my arms uncrossing as my black wings twitched. My abdomen tightened at the sight of her…and then a sharp lash of annoyance followed.

I would never admit—not even to myself—that I'd been looking for her at the market, that a curl of disappointment had spiraled tight in my chest when I'd found her missing from her usual place.

The auburn-haired human woman looked perturbed as she pulled her cart behind her. There was a streak of brown mud across her cheek, and I saw that the wheel of her cart was sticking. She muscled it over a fallen tree limb that cut across the road into the village, nearly stumbling, and I knew why she was late. The Black Veil would not be kind in this weather, the earth sodden and spongy, as if it wanted to pull the living beneath it.

Her hair was damp, like she'd just bathed, and the stray fantasy filtered through my mind before I could stop it. I wondered what she'd look like drying her hair by a roaring fire in the hearth, flames warming her skin, a few stray droplets from her bath trailing down her back. I imagined tracing them with my tongue, making her shiver.

Enough, I thought, gritting my jaw.

From what I'd gathered during brief conversations with the villagers, her name was Marion. Marion Liss, though most children who'd grown up orphans on Allavar almost never kept *Liss* in their names when they became of age.

My lips twitched when I caught her muttered curse, even as far away as I was. When she cleared the fallen branch, she whacked the bolt on the wheel with the edge of her boot. It squealed as she continued to trudge down the road, drawing others' gazes. I watched as she ducked her head, keeping her eyes firmly on the ground in front of her.

My gaze tracked her as I leaned back against the apothecary, relaxing into the stone. I liked the rain—we didn't have it in the Below. The first time I'd felt it on my skin, I'd marveled at how light it felt. And the smell in the Black Veil when it rained? It was a unique earthiness that reminded me of Aeysara's Caves of the Fallen, a place my father had frequented when I'd been younger. It was nothing more than a beautiful tomb…and yet I'd found peace there.

Marion stopped at her usual place, her neighboring vendors having anticipated her arrival and leaving her enough space.

Twenty-three tables now, I thought, watching as she unfolded the rickety, hinged thing, setting its thin legs down into the mud. She frowned down at her boots as they squelched and then smoothed her cloth—inky blue like a midnight cosmia bloom— over the table.

I watched as she pulled dark-colored vials and rounded bottles—green and brown in color—and black jars with stoppered metal lids. Silver wax, shining and smooth, sealed every last one, having dripped down the sides before it'd dried into place.

At the first hint of Marion's wares, villagers began to approach, their pace quickening when they saw others do the same. By the time she unpacked the last bottle, there was a line stretching like a serpent down the road. I watched as she flashed that soft smile, exchanging money with a graceful hand. Her actions were unhurried, but she didn't encourage small talk like some of her nearby vendors. She kept the line moving until she served the last one...and I watched, transfixed.

It should've alarmed me that I was unable to look away from her. Even from this distance I could smell her. Her scent made venom flood over my tongue, beguiling and sweet.

My skin began to itch.

"Trouble sleeping, Lorik Ravael?" came a voice to my left. Slowly, I turned my head. Rysana. Her mouth appeared too wide when she smiled, her gray eyes glittering like the drizzle of the day. "Or perhaps you need salve to heal all your scars? I hear she's a gifted witch, with many little potions to help soothe one's demons."

I chuffed out a short breath. "What are you doing here? I thought you slunk off to Olimara long ago."

"I found work here," Rysana told me, lifting one shoulder. "Can't be too choosy in the Above. You like the witch? I've seen you watching her."

I pushed away from the wall of the apothecary, finding it concerning that I hadn't noticed Rysana in the village before now. Alarming, even. Was I too absorbed with the human woman that I was losing my sense?

Leaning closer to Rysana, I watched as her eyes widened. *Good.* Even here, she knew to be afraid.

"Your glamour is slipping, Rysana," I said, gently like I would to a lover, brushing the backs of my claws over the edge of her lips. She scowled, but I saw her mouth shrink slightly, appearing more suited to her smaller features. I smiled, flashing my fangs. "Diligence. Our king would have no choice but to summon you back home. I'll be watching."

"He has no power here," she said, turning on her heel. I

didn't watch her go, but her lingering words made me feel restless. I made a mental note to report that Rysana was living in Rolara.

Marion's line had dwindled down to nothing, only a few bottles remaining on her table. Like I was tethered, she drew me to her. My booted feet squelched in the mud. There was a buzzing ache building under my skin.

I shouldn't do this, I thought, my fists balling at my sides.

But then her brown eyes lifted. Our gazes collided. I knew that there was no going back now. The choice had been taken from me with the briefest of glimpses.

There was a red flush on the edges of her cheeks when I stopped at her table. But if it was from the cold or my sudden presence, I couldn't be certain. The front of my thighs pressed into the flimsy wood, but it was a barrier between us that I was grateful for.

For a moment, I could only look at her. There was a heaviness in my skull, and it throbbed, perfectly synced, with my heartbeat. My pupils dilated, making the dreary day appear brighter, luminous, and I could see the streaks of bronze in her irises.

For a moment, I felt like I couldn't speak. A tongue-tied boy with her scent filtering through my nostrils, words lodged in my throat like I'd swallowed stones.

Then…the edges of my lips curled and it felt I could breathe again.

"I've seen a lot of vendors at different market days throughout Allavar," I said, placing one palm flat on the table to lean forward. I heard her breath hitch, heard the sound when she swallowed hard. "You are by far the most popular. Not even the female in Olimara who sold ice puffs during the heat wave had a line as long as yours."

"Ice…puffs?" she repeated slowly, her gaze rapt on me. I sensed wariness inlaid with curiosity, puzzlement warring with reservation.

"Ever had them, little witch?" I asked, watching her full lips part. The sweep of her dark lashes fluttered low. The color of her cheeks darkened, and the smile tugged harder at my mouth. "They melt on your tongue like a snowflake, but their sweetness lingers for hours."

Her lashes swept up in a quick motion, and the sear of her eyes made it difficult to breathe. The muscles in my thighs tightened, my left wing twitching at the joint at my back—pulsing with the heartbeat I spied on the column of her neck.

"No," she murmured. "I can't say I ever have. I don't make it a habit to travel to Olimara, especially during heat waves."

My spine straightened. Her saucy remark was surprisingly flippant. I *liked* it. I had to bite back the grin that would've had my fangs flashing in the drizzle.

"And I imagine that something with a name like ice puffs wouldn't last a step beyond that village," she added, her shoulders shrugging, a small smile skirting over her face before her eyes lowered again. I watched them take account of her remaining vials and bottles. "Did you need something in particular?"

My mind flashed back to the fantasy of her in front of the hearth, her auburn wavy hair beginning to curl at the ends as it dried.

Enough.

I blinked hard, refocusing.

"I'm afraid I only have sleeping potions left," she continued, pinching the neck of a slim green bottle to show me, its silver wax seal flashing. "A swig before bed and you'll wonder how you ever slept before it."

"Dangerous, don't you think?" I asked, eyeing the thickened contents sloshing inside. "Maybe that's why you have such a long line every market day. They forget how to sleep without you and your pretty potions. They—you—become an addiction."

Marion frowned, a small down turning of her lips. She placed the bottle back on the table with a small thud.

"If that were the case, I wouldn't have any left, don't you think?" she told me, the brief flash of her wry smile stunning. The last three words mocked the ones I'd used moments before.

Fuck. I even liked it when she sassed me.

I swallowed. "I'll take it."

Her smile never dropped. "Excellent. That'll be thirty *ryn*."

"Aren't they usually twenty-five?" I asked, patting down my vest pocket, feeling the hard square chips of stone there. Allavari black orynx, a precious gemstone mined from the northern stretch of the Massadian Mountains.

"For you, thirty," came her reply, softened with the delicate edge of her smile. "It's late, and I'm nearly out of potions. Wouldn't want the villagers to feel slighted, especially in their terrible state of addiction. It might upset them."

My laugh was low and husky as I handed over three squares of *ryn*. "The extra five *ryn* is your hazard fee? In case of an uprising? An angry mob?"

"Exactly."

She plucked the money from between my fingertips. Our hands brushed. My thumb stroked along hers, just once, and I heard her sharp intake of air.

There was a strange look in her eyes. Wild and uncertain and excited. Like there was a part of her that couldn't believe she was speaking with me this way. Like a part of her didn't recognize herself.

Or maybe she doesn't know who she truly is, came the stray thought. This little witch in the woods, the only Rolarian who dared to live in the Black Veil. All alone. Hiding away? From what?

I wanted to know everything. Everything about her. I was greedy for any new scrap she fed me. It was a discomforting place to be for someone like me…in the thrall of this new obsession. I couldn't understand it because it didn't make sense.

But I wasn't my father, who lived his life tethered to law and logic. He would never bear a crime marking. Not a single one. His honor and virtue would not allow it. It would be a small death to him.

Me? I understood that there were deep folds within the pages of this life, that sometimes those pages were torn or wrinkled or stained or ripped apart at their very seams. I understood that sometimes one needed to bend the law and that a crime didn't make you an evil being. Life was not black and white. Instead it was like a crystal with many faceted sides that were shadowed one moment and glittering the next, depending on the cast of the light.

Marion was brightly lit before me, her eyes glittering like crystals…but I feared I might cast her into shadow one day if I wasn't careful. If I was reckless.

Even still, I stayed, the front of my thighs pressed to the edge of her table. I'd paid for the sleeping potion, and yet I didn't reach for it. Our eyes were holding. Her tantalizing scent made venom drip on my tongue, sweet like ice puffs from Olimara.

I wondered what her blood would taste like, silken and hot and deliciously satisfying. I wondered what her lips would taste like.

My fangs pricked into my bottom lip, and I took a sudden step back. Behind me, my wings flared, and I feared that I'd been so consumed by her that I might've dropped my glamour for a brief moment. But she gave no indication that she'd seen my true face, so my wings tucked against my back, relaxing.

Hypocrite, I thought, seeing as I'd just reprimanded Rysana for the same thing.

Behind me, someone bumped into my shoulder as they skirted around me. An older human male.

"I'll take all the sleeping potions you have left," said the man, a note of desperation in his voice that had me smirking at the human beauty over his head. *See?* I thought, smug. Marion caught my eye. The look was disapproving, but I swore I caught the pull of a smile.

"Of course, Silas," she replied. "I have five left. One hundred twenty *ryn*."

Only twenty-five *ryn* each for him, then. Not thirty.

"Oh," Silas said, reaching a trembling hand into his pocket. The square chips in his palm as he counted them carefully made Marion's lips press. He was short. "Only four bottles, on second thought."

Marion pushed over five, and Silas began to protest.

"Take them," Marion insisted as she took the *ryn* from his outstretched hand. "You're doing me a favor. Now I can leave sooner. You know the village always makes me restless."

"I'll pay you the rest next month," he promised.

"Please, don't," she replied, embarrassed.

Silas frowned, but his eyes were already on the five bottles. He had a brown cloth bag slung over his shoulder, and he began to nestle the potions inside. Distracted, he almost took mine, but my hand flashed out, snagging it quickly.

He looked at me, startled, his mouth agape. I grinned. My fangs flashed. "That one's mine."

I had no use for sleeping potions. Yet there was an alarming part of me that wanted something of hers. Something that she'd made. Something that she'd poured her time and talents into.

"My apologies," Silas murmured, nodding at Marion quickly in appreciation and then scurrying away.

I was still grinning when I looked back to Marion.

Her brow was raised. "Possessive, aren't you?"

My smile widened. I looked down to the potion bottle, its content sloshing inside when I shook it. Something shimmered within it like starlight. *Glowfly magic*, I realized.

"You have no idea," I rasped, catching her eyes once more.

Her table was empty now. She was free to leave, just as she'd claimed she wanted. But her feet were rooted into place like the ancient river trees in the Black Veil, whose trunks were so wide that they seemed like small mountains, immovable and eternal.

It was on the tip of my tongue to ask her to Grimstone's for an Allavari ale. Wasn't that what these villagers did to court one another? I wanted to look into her glittering eyes in a dark back booth and listen to her voice. I wondered what would make her laugh or if those were as hard to come by as her smiles.

I wanted to steal her kiss and feel her whispered sigh across my tongue.

Instead I took another step away, feeling the weight of the potion in my palm.

"Take caution on your way home," I told her, nodding my head to the entrance of the Black Veil.

Her lashes lowered, and she began to ball up her table cloth. "Thank you for your concern. But I don't really believe in all the stories the villagers whisper about. The Severs in there have always steered clear of me."

My throat tightened. "You should believe them. There is always some truth in stories."

Marion's hand paused, and she looked up at me again. Just then, I felt a searing heat at my inner wrist. I looked down, saw the mark appear, shimmering across my skin.

"Have a good evening, little witch," I said, the edge of my lip curling.

Then I turned away, my palm gripping the rounded bottle tight enough that I thought I might shatter it.

No good will come from this, I reminded myself, my jaw gritting.

The mark at my wrist tingled like a touch. Warm and distracting. I was being summoned home.

The entrance to the Below was nothing more than a hollowed-out tree trunk. Once, it had been splintered from within by black fire, an ancient spell cast by Veranis Sarin. Other portals had been created over the years, spread out across Allavar, but this was my preferred entrance. The closest to home and nestled deep within the confines of the Black Veil, where very few dared to venture.

I pushed the little witch from my mind and stepped into the tree. The magic shot through me like a spear of lightning, and I breathed deep, feeling my shoulders relax. I pressed my fingertips into the blackened, deadened bark, answering the call with magic of my own. *Reciprocity.* The Below gave to me, and so I gave to it. I felt the energy spread from beneath my own hand, like ink over wet parchment.

The portal veil was like the gossamer wings of a glowfly. Delicate and light and pierced easily. When I felt it split, I stepped through.

The air was pure and crisp. I would never get tired of that first deep breath of home.

I let my glamour drop as the magic surged in, filling my lungs, wrapping around my bones. My strength returned in a dizzying rush, and I wanted to bellow at the relief.

Once I caught my breath, I stepped from the portal. The Sarin Woods spread around me, serene and hushed. Behind me, there wasn't a deadened trunk like in the Black Veil. Instead I stepped from Sarin's Temple, made of alabaster Aeysarian stone, the strands of silver ore weaving through it like glittering thread. In moonlight, the small temple glowed like a beacon.

The sun was nearly gone beyond the trees, and I cut through to the river path which would lead me into Aeysara, the Below King's city.

As I walked farther, the gentle trickle of the stream crescendoed into the violent rush of a river. The soft and spongy forest floor became unyielding paved road. The sky darkened. When I neared the south bridge into Aeysara, I heard the roar of the waterfall as it tumbled into the great sea below the city.

The blue lights were beginning to glow in their glass lanterns along the bridge, casting pools of light at my feet. Stray glowflies—brightbell glowflies, perhaps—flittered across the bridge. A hive must've been nearby, perhaps tucked next to the river.

The gray cobbled stone clattered beneath my boots. I saw a tall figure standing at the end of the bridge. Someone I didn't expect to see here.

"What are you doing down here?" I asked, approaching the Kelvarian male. I frowned, noticing we were alone. "Without a guard?"

The Below King rested his arms against the ledge, peering down at the lake beyond. The waterfall tumbled right below us, the river's path ending at the bridge, and it cast spray upward, misting the air. I blinked it away from my eyes, turning my back to lean against the banister.

"Am I not allowed to walk within my city?" he asked. His lips curled, and he cast me a sideways glance, his silver eyes catching the rising moon. "May I remind you, Lorik Ravael, that I was like you once? Free to come and go as I pleased, without needing to answer to anyone."

"You were not the king then," I said simply, crossing my arms over my chest, the sleeping potion still hanging loosely from my grip. "And my father will not be happy you are unaccompanied, given the..."

I trailed off, and the Below King looked at me knowingly, almost daring me to continue.

"Given the disturbances of late," I finished.

His eyes lowered, the line of his mouth thinning for a brief moment.

"What is that?" he asked, nodding at the bottle in my possession.

"A sleeping potion," I answered, bringing it up to my eyes and giving it a shake. Blue sparks glowed brightly within before they faded.

"Having trouble sleeping, Ravael? A week or two home might help cure that."

Hadn't Rysana asked me the same thing?

I sighed and turned, scanning the bridge and the path from Sarin Woods I'd just come from. I'd seen no Shades and didn't scent any on the road inward either. We were alone. This section of Aeysara was always quiet this late. He knew that. We wouldn't be disturbed here.

"Perhaps I purchased it for you, my king," I said.

"How thoughtful. I might have need of it soon if these *disturbances* continue."

"Why did you summon me?" I asked, watching him carefully. "Has something else happened?"

The Below King turned. There was a lantern between us, and it cast his face in blue light, making his gray skin appear darker. His black wings—the scars silver and thin across them—hung heavy at his back, dragging on the cobblestones. He was wearing a long dark blue tunic, the hem cutting at his knees, a slit running up the side to his hips. Embroidered into the fabric was silver thread, the pattern intricate, hand stitched by an expert seamstress.

His black pants were neat and molded loosely to his legs. Not a single scuff mark marred his silver-toed boots. At his wrists were glittering Aeysarian metal cuffs—a gift from a Kelvarian sorceress when he'd taken the throne, forged and soaked in magic to channel his own power more easily.

Behind him, Aeysara sat, quiet and peaceful, following the path that led from the bridge. The road weaved and swirled across the flat land before heading up the mountain pass and running below along the cliffside, homes built into the rock. The road widened just after the bridge, and there were two statues on either side. Tall and wide and eternal like the river trees in the Black Veil. One was of Veranis Sarin. The other was of his Hunter, the Below King's own bloodline.

"There is a rumor of a sorceress who lives in the Outer Lands," he told me. A chill prickled the back of my neck. "Within the Ashen woodlands. An Alashen sorceress."

"Did Thela tell you this?" I wondered, my tone darkening.

"Yes," he told me. "So has your father."

I straightened, frowning.

"He told me he saw her."

"He did?" I rasped, shock souring my belly. "When? That day?"

"He told me she saved Thela's life with magic he's never seen before. Never felt before."

I processed the words, knowing that if my father had spoken them, they must've been true. I knew that with certainty, though it only brought more questions rising. Why hadn't he ever told me this? Had my mother known? And Thela…

"Thela told me," I started quietly, "that she was mad. That the sorceress spoke to things not there. That she told Thela she had cut the horns away from her mother's and her grandmother's bodies and adhered them to her own head when they died. So they would always be with her."

The Below King's lips pressed together and his chin lowered. "Yes. The Alashen people believe magic flows from their goddess through their horns first. They consider them sacred."

"Then what of the sorceress? She cut her own from her head to replace them with her mother's and grandmother's? Is this really what we've been driven to, Kyavar? To enlist the aid of a witch in the woods, driven mad with grief?"

The Below King held my gaze.

"And what if it is the Alashen doing this to us?" I questioned. "This blood magic, turning our people into Shades, condemning them to a lifeless existence…this kind of power hasn't been seen since Veranis."

"If Alashen magic is responsible, then perhaps Alashen magic is the only way to stop it."

I scoffed, the summoning mark on my wrist burning. Instead of a comfort, it felt like my skin was twisting.

"I have to consider all possibilities," Kyavar murmured. "I know you will understand that. That is why I am tasking you with finding the sorceress, Lorik. I want you to lead a scouting party out at dawn. Don't return to Aeysara until you find her."

I closed my eyes, feeling the mist of the waterfall brush my cheeks. It reminded me of the drizzle in Rolara. It reminded me of Marion, with her damp hair and flushed skin.

"And if she's dead? They encountered her nearly twenty years ago."

"Then bring back her bones," my king ordered. "We lost ten more Aeysarians today. Even more in the villages. They will all become Shades within the week."

When I opened my eyes, I saw he had already turned away. His footsteps echoed on the path that led back into city. Just then, I heard the night chants from the sky temple lift into the sky. Beautiful voices, so ethereal and pure, echoed through the city. So haunting, they pierced me through my chest. The backs of my eyes burned.

"I thought he'd never leave."

I started, peering down over the side of the bridge.

Thela blinked up at me, completely soaked to the bone and shivering. She had tucked herself beneath the bridge, leaning against one of the support columns, situated on a precarious stone ledge right before the waterfall tumbled over the cliff.

"Get up here," I growled. "What if you had gone over the falls?"

"Then I would've swum to the north bank and walked back home," she answered, grinning, wiping the water from her eyes.

Thela had been born without wings, which made her position at the edge of the waterfall all the more concerning.

I leaned over the side of the bridge, my arm outstretched, and she grabbed it. I hauled her up easily, only feeling the tight knot release in my chest when she had her two feet firmly planted. Water dripped off her clothes, making a large pool at her feet.

"What were you thinking?" I asked, my nostrils flaring.

"I was thinking that Father would be upset if Kyavar was unaccompanied."

"Don't call him that," I reprimanded.

"You did," she challenged, raising a brow.

"That's different."

"How? He's your king too."

Stubborn female, I thought.

"If Father finds out you were under the bridge—"

"But he won't, will he?" she asked, her eyes shining as she wrung out her long black hair.

I bit the inside of my cheek, my fist squeezing around the potion bottle.

"You two still act like I'm a child," Thela observed, sighing. She wandered to the banister, taking the same place that the Below King had. She inspected the stone, running her hands across it like she could still feel the heat of his palm there. She stroked the stone like it was his hand. "Do you think you'll ever see me as anything else?"

There was a tendril of hurt in her tone, and it made the anger in my chest deflate like it had been pierced by a needle. Slow but steady.

"I'm the same age our brother was when he died. Older, actually," she continued. My brow furrowed. Had it been that long already? She gave me a sad smile. "Isn't that strange? I realized it the other day, and it nearly brought me to tears."

"Yes," I answered softly, joining her to peer down at the great sea below as the sky temple chants filled the quiet. Our shoulders touched. "Yes, that is strange."

Thela's expression was calm as she regarded me. We studied one another, and I knew what she was thinking.

"I'm not taking you with me," I informed her. "And you know better than to eavesdrop on a conversation between the Below King and his Hunter. If anyone else had discovered you…"

"I didn't expect you to stroll up," she argued, rolling her eyes. "He was here for a long time. And you haven't been home in nearly five days."

"Did you miss me, sister?" I teased.

Thela huffed.

"I *worry* for you," she corrected.

My smile came easily, and I bumped her shoulder with my wing. "What is of danger to me in the Above?"

Her eyes drifted down to the potion bottle in my grip.

"You tell me," she replied, reaching for the bottle.

The back of my neck tingled, and my smile slowly died. Thela always saw far more than she should. She was like our mother in that way.

I watched as she shook the potion, her face lighting up with bright blue before the glowfly magic faded. Her eyes met mine.

"She's talented, whoever she is," she commented, returning the potion. "Does Father know?"

"There's nothing to know," I rasped, frustration coiling in my chest.

"Very well," she said. "I know where the sorceress is—I remember the way. You should take me with you."

"I already said I wouldn't," I told her. "And Father knows the way. In fact, he probably remembers the path better than you. You were only eight years old."

"A child's memory is sometimes better. We absorb more. We *feel* more," she said. "I remember everything. Everything about her. The color of her eyes. The two different shades of her horns, one longer and more curled than the other. Her mother's, I think, that one. The knots in her hair. The way she smelled. She was so very…sad. So sad, Lorik."

Discomfort threaded down my spine, making my wings twitch. "My answer is no, Thela. Don't ask me again."

My sister drew in a deep breath and then released it. "Yes, Hunter."

A sound like a growl made its way up my throat.

"Do you like being in the Above more than being home? Is that why you stay away so long?"

The question was vulnerable, and my brow furrowed. "Of course not. Is that what you think?"

But I thought I tasted the bitter tinge of a lie on my tongue, making me question my answer. *Do I?* I wondered, scowling.

"The Above…it's different. An entirely new experience, an entirely new place—one we've only ever heard about in stories, Thela," I continued. "There are things I like about the Above. Things I don't. Just like home."

"But?"

My lips lifted. I leaned my arms across the banister and let my hand dangle over the edge, the potion bottle swaying.

"*But* being home does have its own responsibilities. They are beginning to weigh heavier. So heavy sometimes it's hard to breathe. I think I've been a coward," I admitted, feeling Thela's hand rest on my forearm, the warmth of her touch comforting and familiar. "Hiding away in the Above when I am needed here most."

The shameful words hurtled from me.

"I have this recurring dream where you leave for the Above and you never come back," Thela admitted quietly. "I worry it will take you away one day."

"Don't *ever* think that," I scolded, my tone harsh. I felt raw from my admission, and hearing my sister's words cut even deeper.

"We would be all right if you decided that," Thela told me. My lips parted, and I swung my head to regard her. A sting of hurt pinched in my chest. Her gaze strayed to the bottle. "If you wanted something more there. If it made you happy, I would forgive you."

I didn't know what it was…this feeling that came over me. I felt like a statue, an eternal river tree, my legs heavy on the bridge. I felt rooted into place like the ancient statues or slotted into the stone of the road beneath my feet.

This is your home, I told myself. *Don't let silly fantasies blind you from duty, from family.*

My fingers relaxed. Thela gasped as she watched the potion bottle disappear over the edge of the waterfall.

She studied me carefully, but I swung my arm around her shoulders and turned her from the bridge, leading her down the familiar road that I'd walked the entirety of my life. As a boy, I'd often sneak into Sarin Woods. Even before I knew how, I'd attempt to open the portal, sitting in Sarin's Temple for hours as the magic floated over me. So frustrating because I couldn't grasp it. Not yet. I hadn't understood the reciprocity of it then.

"Let's go home," I told her.

"You mean that?"

"Yes. I have to be up before dawn to find your sorceress, after all, and now I find myself short of a sleeping potion."

"A river will always find the sea," Thela murmured, her hand patting mine. "Though there are many twists and turns in between."

"I haven't heard that in many years," I commented quietly, my eyes casting down onto the paved road. Something our grandmother had always said.

"I think about it every day," Thela told me.

We passed between the statues of Veranis Sarin and his

Hunter. There was a break in song from the sky temple, and Aeysara was blissfully quiet, the golden lights in the distance twinkling. Welcoming.

"Your potion will wash up on the bank by the morning," Thela told me, giving me a sly smile. "Things meant for you will always find their way back to you. And knowing you, Lorik… you'll find it just fine."

NEWSLETTER

Want to hear about new releases, exclusive giveaways, and get access to bonus content, like extended epilogues and character art?

Sign up for Zoey Draven's newsletter:

If you're already subscribed to my newsletter, access all bonus content here:

https://zoeydraven.com/bonus-content/

CONNECT WITH ZOEY
SCAN THE QR CODE WITH YOUR PHONE TO ACCESS HER LINKS:

I'M MOSTLY HANGING OUT ON INSTAGRAM. COME SAY HI!

ABOUT THE AUTHOR

Zoey Draven has been writing stories for as long as she can remember. Her love affair with the romance genre started with her grandmother's old Harlequin paperbacks and has continued ever since. As an Amazon Top 50 bestselling author, now she gets to write the happily-ever-afters—with an otherworldly twist, of course! She is the author of Sci-Fi and Fantasy Romance books, such as the *Horde Kings of Dakkar* and the *Brides of the Kylorr* series.

When she's not writing, she's probably drinking one too many cups of coffee, hiking in the redwoods, or spending time with her family.

Website: www.ZoeyDraven.com
Facebook group: Zoey's Reader Zone

Made in United States
Orlando, FL
13 March 2025